Guns Along the Jicarilla

**Center Point
Large Print**

**This Large Print Book carries the
Seal of Approval of N.A.V.H.**

Guns Along the Jicarilla

Ray Hogan

Center Point Publishing
Thorndike, Maine

This Center Point Large Print edition
is published in the year 2004 by arrangement with
Golden West Literary Agency.

The text of this Large Print edition is unabridged. In other
aspects, this book may vary from the original edition. Printed in
Thailand. Set in 16-point Times New Roman type by
Bill Coskrey and Gary Socquet.

ISBN 1-58547-384-7

Library of Congress Cataloging-in-Publication Data

Hogan, Ray, 1908-
    Guns along the Jicarilla / Ray Hogan.--Center Point large print ed.
        p. cm.
    ISBN 1-58547-384-7 (lib. bdg. : alk. paper)
    1. Large type books. I. Title.

PS3558.O3473G814 2004
813'.54--dc22

LP
Hogan

2003060277

❈ I ❈

JIM HOLT swung down slowly from the sorrel gelding, stood for a time in the hot, streaming sunlight and studied the building before him. The Palace Saloon, a new sign on the recently painted front of the structure advised him. He grunted in surprise. Here was change. Five years ago, the place had been called the Sidewinder, and looked nothing at all like it did now.

Wrapping the sorrel's leathers around the hitchrack bar, he turned lazily on his heel to survey the remainder of Butte's single street. A big man, well over six feet with weight to match, he had dark hair worn somewhat long, deep set, shadowed eyes and a hard, straight slash for a mouth.

As he came about, his muscular body seemed to flow beneath the lightweight trail clothing he wore, and the hand that hung level with the pistol slung at his hip appeared large, almost hamlike. But there was a deceptive grace to his movements, one that suggested swiftness and readiness, and laid a faint aura of danger upon him.

Five years. . . . Little else had altered in Butte. The Cattleman's Bank . . . Mason's Feed & Grain store . . . the Paramount Hotel . . . Buckman's General Store . . . Reece Oatman, Loans & Real Estate. . . . Jim's glance came to a stop on the small office next to Jackson's Barber Shop.

Oatman had been a rancher five years ago. He had

owned a small spread at the southern edge of the Jicarilla Basin, a few miles below Wade McClendon's
where Jim had worked for a spell. Oatman had been
only a so-so rancher, never really much good at it. Evidently he had finally realized he might do better in a
different line of business and sold out.

All else seemed the same—dusty, weather-beaten,
sun-bleached, and he guessed that was as it should be.
Progress was slow, particularly in a Territory as new,
even though ancient, as New Mexico. A man couldn't
expect things to change much.

Reversing himself, he stepped up onto the saloon's
porch, crossed to the open doorway, and entered. His
lengthy stride was smooth and effortless as a cat's.
Five men were at the bar—all strangers. The bartender
he didn't know either. There was no one at the tables.
Holt's practiced eye took it all in with a quick,
sweeping probe as he crossed to the long counter.

Conversation among the patrons ceased at his
appearance. He felt their cool appraisal, curious and
calculating, and then saw them turn back to their
drinks. One wore the town marshal's star. An old man
with white hair and a trailing mustache. Jim gave him
a second glance; he did look vaguely familiar.

"What'll it be?"

Holt rested his elbows on the counter, faced the
aproned man. "Whiskey," he said.

The bartender reached for a bottle and glass, poured.

"Leave it," Jim said, nodding at the bottle. "Been a
long day." He was aware then, of the attention being
placed upon him by one of the riders at the bar—a tall,

6

husky blond with thick shoulders. He met the puncher's glance with a flat stare, let it hold until the blond turned away, then brought his attention back to the bartender.

"This place got a new owner?"

The man behind the counter shrugged. "Jess Hammer's been running it for a year, more or less."

Jess Hammer. . . . He'd been a gambler working the tables when Charlie Case was the proprietor. Case, like Oatman, must have sold out and gone looking for greener pastures; that, or he had lost the place to Hammer in a high-stakes card game.

"Business must be pretty good," Holt said, looking over the new furnishings, the well stocked shelves. "Reckon Jess's as good a saloonman as he was a gambler."

"We're doing all right," the bartender answered. "It's two bits a shot for what you're drinking."

"I'll keep count," Jim said.

"So'll I," the bar man commented drily, and moved down the counter to where his other customers stood.

Holt eased around, slumped comfortably with his elbows hooked on the edge of the bar. It was good to be off the saddle, inside, out of the sun. The ride from Fort Sumner had been long, hot—one he'd as soon not been asked to make.

Wade McClendon's letter had not said much, only that he had need of his services and would be obliged if he came. McClendon was that way. He never was one to waste words; but by that very fact, Jim knew the rancher was in bad trouble of some sort, and would not

7

have written the letter at all if it hadn't been something serious. He had accordingly taken to the saddle and headed for Butte and the Jicarilla Basin the next day after the letter arrived.

Idly he wondered just what kind of a problem McClendon had on his hands. Five years ago it had been homesteaders. It wouldn't be that again; the sodbusters had learned the hard way that the Basin was not farming land, that it was fit only for grazing cattle.

Rustlers, possibly. When ranchers in an area started to prosper and do well, rustlers always began to move in like ants at a Sunday picnic. . . . Of course it could be no more than some sort of hell-raising the ranchers and the local lawman couldn't cope with.

Whatever it was, was serious; otherwise McClendon wouldn't have called him in. No one ever sent for a fast gun just to pass the time of day—not that he resented such, particularly. It was a pretty easy way of life, and it paid a hell of a lot better than tailing-up steers.

Some sort of a noisy argument had developed among the men at the bar; loud talking, swearing, laughing. Jim pivoted his attention to that direction. The old marshal was pocketed in the center of the younger men, his back to the counter. Face a glowing red, he was shaking his head stubbornly.

"Aw, come on, Marshal, show us you're the big man you're claiming to be!" It was the redhead speaking. He was holding a near-full bottle of whiskey in his hand, trying to force it on the lawman.

The punchers were all pretty drunk; the big blond perhaps least of any, or showing it less than the others,

8

maybe. The tough-faced, dark man to his left had a fixed grin on his lips, and the youngest of them—the boy with the Texas twang in his voice—had a wild, eager look in his eyes.

"Only right," he drawled. "You're awanting us to swallow that yarn about how good a shooter you was. Way to prove it is to show us how good a drinker you are." He glanced at the blond. "Ain't that right, Cully?"

The blond rider nodded. "He does, I'll sure believe him. But he's got to drink the whole quart without stopping."

The marshal continued to shake his head. The one with the red hair nodded to the Texan and the dark faced man. "Grab hold of his arm, Billy Jay. You too, Earl. I'll just pour it down him."

The bartender came to life. "Now, hold on, Reno. Jess don't like no ruckusing in—"

"The hell with what Jess don't like!" Reno snapped. "Cully, grab him by the hair—"

The lawman jerked back, flinging a despairing look at Holt as he tried to twist away. Jim set his glass on the counter, moved silently toward the struggling group. Catching Reno by the shoulder, he spun the redhead around, slapped the bottle from his grasp and sent it crashing to the floor.

"Fun's over," he said softly.

Cully whirled on him. "Who the hell you think you are?"

"I'm the one horning in," Holt said. "Now you and your playmates move on; leave the marshal be."

The old lawman hurriedly pulled himself out of the

9

center of the group. Reno, his balance regained, squared himself and now stood spraddle-legged glaring at Holt.

"Mister, maybe you've horned in once too many. Could be you've bit yourself off a chunk you ain't going to find easy chewing."

"Reckon I'll manage," Jim answered, easing away from the bar.

"My, he sure is a big one!" Billy Jay said in his slow, lazy way.

"Don't mean nothing," Reno said. "Only makes more racket when he falls."

Abruptly he lunged. Holt anticipated the move, started a short, right-hand swing that met the rider head on. Reno jolted in mid-stride, quivered, and staggered back, his face slightly green.

In that same instant, Cully and Billy Jay made their move. Rushing, they sought to trap Jim between them. Holt, sidestepping neatly, caught the young Texan by one arm and flung him sprawling into the nearby tables. He felt Cully's balled fist drive into his ribs, recoiled to absorb the power of the blow. Throwing up a forearm, he blocked an oncoming right and smashed the tall blond hard on the nose.

Cully rocked back on his heels, caught himself, charged in again. He was game, Jim thought. Usually one wallop like that ended a fight. He jerked back, allowed the puncher to miss, then whipped a stinging left into Cully's middle, a sharp right to the jaw. Cully went to his hands and knees.

Billy Jay was up, crouched, watching angrily. He

seemed unsure as to whether or not he wanted to mix in further. On the floor, Reno—both hands clutched to his belly—was staring dazedly into space. Only the darkly silent rider called Earl had made no move.

Holt gave him a small, quiet smile. "Your turn," he murmured.

Earl shook his head. "Not my way," he said, and dropped his hand toward the pistol at his hip.

Holt's forty-five appeared as if by magic. Earl froze, eyes narrowing as a deep frown creased his forehead.

"Now, wait—"

"You called it," Jim said. "I'll holster and we'll start over again."

Earl's glance dropped. He shook his head, and hands well away from his weapon, moved slowly toward Reno. Reaching down, he caught the rider under the arms, helped him to his feet.

Jim Holt drew back, once more hooked his elbows on the edge of the bar. At once, Billy Jay crossed to Cully, started to assist him. The tall rider angrily shook off the Texan, got up under his own power.

Wordlessly, he swept Holt with a furious glance and moved toward the door, his three companions trailing after him. Jim waited until they had reached their horses, mounted, and were wheeling away, before turning to the lawman.

"Can't say as I admire the kind of friends you pick, Marshal."

"Ain't no friends of mine," the lawman snapped. "Was I looking to—"

"Then who are they?"

11

"Cowhands, from one of the big ranches in the Basin. One's Cully Ryan. He's the ramrod for Wade McClendon at the Circle X. Others—Joe Reno, Billy Jay Austin and Earl Munger—they work there, too."

❊ II ❊

JIM HOLT groaned softly. McClendon's foreman and some of his crew. He might have known; luck always seemed to start him off on the wrong foot. But he was a little surprised that McClendon would have such men as those working for him—especially Munger who definitely was a gunslinger, and the red-headed Joe Reno who was nothing more than a saddlebum and a troublemaker. Cully Ryan did appear to be a cut above the others, he had to admit. Likely it was the liquor inside him that made him proddy.

"You just passing through?" the old marshal asked, stepping aside so that the bartender could sweep and mop up the shattered bottle of whiskey.

"Mostly," Holt replied. "That kind of treatment of the law usual around here?"

The marshal shrugged. "I'm used to it. Ain't much I could do, anyway. Law don't mean nothing to folks."

"Sort of leaves the gate open for Reno and his kind, don't it?"

"Reckon so, but you see I ain't no real lawman. We ain't never had no bad trouble in this town, and folks don't figure there's any need of paying out a lot of money for a big-time, fancy badge-toter. So when I closed up my livery stable, they hung this star on me

12

and started giving me twenty-five dollars a month and keep.

"Wasn't supposed to do no lawing, just walk around so's outsiders could see the town had a marshal."

Holt was remembering. . . . The mention of the livery stable had brought it back to him. The old man's name was Pete Hornbuckle. He'd been around Butte for a long time.

"Heard there was trouble around here now," Jim said, feeling his way. "That star might start meaning something."

The bartender had finished his chore, was moving in behind the counter. Jim motioned for a new bottle, pointing to his glass and that of Hornbuckle. The lawman waited until his drink had been poured, lifted the small glass, and downed the liquor in a single gulp. Then he bobbed his head.

"Obliged. Sure don't mind drinking with friendly folks. . . . Yeh, we got us some trouble aplenty out in the Basin. Lot of rustling going on. Plain meanness, too, like burning down line shacks and barns. One of the ranchers got hisself held up a while back. Lost a right smart amount of cash he was carrying."

"And you don't have to worry about it?"

Hornbuckle stroked his mustache. "For twenty-five a month I ain't expected to do nothing but stand around. Real lawing is somebody else's business. Fact is, they already got some high-faluting gunny coming in to take charge. Hell on a pair of lightning rods, I'm told. Friend of McClendon's. Worked for him about five, six years ago when they had a spell of trouble out there.

Don't recollect his name. Can't remember much, like I used to."

Holt didn't feel the necessity for filling in the gaps in the old man's memory; such could take place later. He'd learned long ago that considerable advantage lay in being unknown.

Draining his glass, he set it aside, reached into his pocket for change and glanced questioningly at the bartender.

"Be a dollar," the man said, and then added, "Thanks," when Holt dropped a coin onto the counter.

Jim turned to the lawman. "Been a pleasure meeting you, Marshal. Hope to see you again."

Hornbuckle, his slight figure dwarfed alongside Holt, extended his hand hastily. "Been a pleasure for me too. And I'm real obliged for you stepping in when you did. That Reno can just about hooraw a man to pieces, once he gets started."

"Next time use that gun you're wearing on him," Jim said, moving for the door. "Sometimes you've got to shoot a man like him to teach others a lesson."

Hornbuckle's jaw sagged. "Why, I sure couldn't do that. Not me. I ain't supposed—"

"You keep wearing that star and you may have to," Holt said, and passed on through the opening onto the porch.

He crossed to the sorrel and stood for a brief time staring at Butte's only restaurant. He debated the advisability of eating his evening meal there and then heading out for McClendon's Circle X. He wasn't actually hungry, he decided, and it was still fairly early—a couple of hours until sundown, at least. He guessed he'd just ride on, eat at McClendon's.

Swinging onto the sorrel, he cut about, rode down the street to where it forked, and veered onto the west branch. He let his glance range on ahead. The country looked good, rich, and green despite the fact that it was late summer. Evidently there had been a fine spring, one with plenty of rain.

He liked the Jicarilla Basin, had even considered staying there, starting up a place of his own. The winters were never too bad and you could always depend upon the deep snows of the Colorado mountains to the north to keep the Jicarilla River and the lesser creeks flowing clear and strong. There was plenty of grass for everyone, along with a surplus of open range over which there'd never been a dispute among the six ranchers who occupied the vast swale.

He probably would have remained, he supposed, if that homesteader trouble hadn't arisen. He'd been a working cowhand for McClendon at the time, and somehow had gotten pushed by the rancher into taking charge of the whole affair.

That was what had spoiled it all for him insofar as ranching was concerned. He discovered he possessed a flair for handling trouble, and that along with a natural talent for using his fists and a startling adeptness with a pistol—none of which he had ever taken particular note until called upon—had opened a new way of life for him.

And so he had ridden out after the trouble was over, and a reputation had ridden with him. He found himself being looked up and called upon to do jobs that to him seemed more or less ordinary; in reality they were tasks requiring not only full use of the skills he had but ice-cold nerve as well.

Now he was back in the country he had liked so well and he wondered if he would leave it again when he'd finished. He had no answer as he looked out over the smooth, grass-covered hills that bubbled off into the distance, melted into what was the Jicarilla Basin proper.

What would happen, would happen; and what was in a man's mind today could be gone tomorrow. He put the thought aside. It was just good to lope on through the fading heat of the afternoon, soak in the familiar sights, recall the land.

Unless there'd been a change, Jack Bevan's Cross Bar ranch would be to his right, the first spread inside the Basin on its eastern side. Directly north of him lay Damion King, and at the far, upper end of the huge hollow would be Carl Johnson's C Bar J outfit.

Hans Kastner, the moon-faced German who had begat seven daughters in his quest for a single son, would be south of that on the west side. Then came a broad expanse of open range used by all—the area in which he had considered placing his own spread.

At the foot of the western border was McClendon's Circle X—not as large in land measure as Carl Johnson's ranch—but much greater in the size and number of herds, its buildings, and crew.

Farther on to the south and well below McClendon, placed at the very lip of the Basin, was Reece Oatman's place. It was the smallest and poorest of them all; but it could be made to pay if a man used his head, grazed his cattle to the west, and did a little planting for supplemental hay.

On a spur notion Holt decided he'd look into the Oatman place. If Reece had simply given up ranching, abandoned the property, he just might take it over—try his hand at beef raising.

Jim Holt grinned as the sorrel loped on steadily. Who the hell was he trying to fool? Slaving away from daylight to dark, fighting the heat in summer, the cold in winter, drought, unexpected blizzards, range fires, cow fever, rustlers. Not for him! He'd found out five years ago there was a better life; he'd be a *burro loco* to go back to the old way.

Ahead he caught the silver flicker of water. Jicarilla River. . . . He'd covered the distance from town in a lot faster time than he'd realized. McClendon's was only a short distance beyond the stream. He'd be glad to get there. The damned saddle was beginning to feel like a part of him.

He forded the Jicarilla, noting that it was up to the gelding's belly—high for so late in the summer—and climbed out onto the opposite bank. Bright splashes of flowers were everywhere; faded purple phlox, vivid red paintbrush, brightly smiling fleabane, and the always present sunflower with its small cousin, the crownbeard. Grass was tall and lush. For a moment he was tempted to halt, wipe the sweat from his face, and enjoy the coolness.

But he rejected the idea, continued on down the well-marked road. He jumped a mule-deer buck in the grove of cottonwoods through which he passed a short time later, paused briefly to watch its graceful flight through the dappling of shadows, and pressed on. Somewhere among the spreading trees a dove was mourning, and high above in the spotless blue sky an eagle soared effortlessly on its broad wings.

He broke out of the grove onto a narrow, little flat that he remembered well: a place where he had met, and had a showdown with, two gunmen the homesteaders had hired. He saw the buildings that made up McClendon's ranch a quarter mile distant.

There were a couple of new ones, and the barn had been enlarged. He was surprised at the way the trees around the place had grown, at the several banks of flowers bordering the edges of the yard, and recalled the old saw: *In this country even the rocks will grow if given water.* He could almost believe it.

Reaching the gate with its chain-suspended sign bearing only the Circle X brand, Holt allowed the sorrel to walk slowly across the grassy sod toward the main house on the left.

He heard a door slam, turned to see Cully Ryan (with a half a dozen men in tow) come onto the hardpack in long, angry strides hurrying to intercept him. Sighing, Holt drew to a stop.

McClendon's ramrod, his face somewhat swollen, halted half a dozen steps away. Billy Jay and Munger were in the group. The others, Jim had not seen before.

"If you're looking for work," Ryan said in an iron-hard voice, "turn around and get out. Ain't no job around here for you."

❊ III ❊

H OLT CONSIDERED the rider thoughtfully. Raising a hand, he again wiped sweat from his brow and said mildly, "Pull in your horns, cowboy. McClendon hired me."

Surprise flared in Ryan's eyes. "The hell he did! Never said nothing to me about it."

"Maybe he don't tell you everything," Holt said, and touching the sorrel lightly with his spurs, rode on.

Ryan swore harshly, took a long step forward, and halted as McClendon's voice cut through the sudden hush.

"Forget it, Cully. He's a friend of mine."

The rancher, accompanied by another man, had come out onto the porch of the house. A broad smile was on his lips.

"Howdy, Jim! When I heard about a scrap in town and got a look at Cully and the boys that was with him, I figured you'd arrived. . . . Step down."

Holt pulled to a halt at the hitchrack, stepped from the saddle and, moving up onto the gallery, clasped the rancher's hand. "Good to see you, Wade."

McClendon turned to the man behind him. "You remember Jack Bevan, I expect."

Holt extended his hand to meet that of the rancher. Bevan was older, more settled looking. About time. . . . Jack had been a bit on the wild side five years ago. McClendon reached for the door knob, glanced over his shoulder at the men in the yard.

"Cully, reckon you ought to be in on this. Rest of you go on about your work."

The foreman hesitated, said something to the rider nearest him, and then moved toward the porch. McClendon, holding open the screen door, ushered the three men into the parlor of the house.

"Damned if you ain't bigger'n you was the last time I saw you," he said to Jim. "You ever figure to stop growing?"

The rancher let the screen slam with a bang, looked toward the back of the house and shouted, "Mother, you got any more of that lemonade?" before wrestling several of the heavy, cowhide-covered chairs into a circle.

"Sit down, sit down," he rumbled when all was to his satisfaction. Again he glanced to the rear of the place and yelled, "Mother—what about that lemonade?"

Mrs. McClendon, a graying, shy woman appeared almost at once bearing a tray with a pitcher and several glasses. She placed it on a small, carved-leg table, smiled pleasantly to all and withdrew. McClendon immediately filled a glass for each and sank gratefully into one of the chairs.

"Sure glad you're here," he said, raising his glass to Holt. "Good trip?"

"Hot. Miles never get any shorter."

"Longer," the rancher said. "Been finding that out the last few months." He paused, looked slyly at Cully Ryan. "Since you were in town, did you get some idea of what's going on around here?"

"Not much," Holt replied. "Met your marshal."

"Pete? Don't count on him. Sort of a pension job, all it amounts to."

"Maybe the town ought to hire on a better lawman if it don't figure he's good enough. Might keep things going right for you here in the Basin."

"A thought," McClendon said. "Always been able to handle things ourselves—leastwise up to now. But things are changing. We're all getting bigger and the ranchers don't seem to work together like they used to. We were kind of like a team of horses then, all pulling for the common good. Now—"

Bevan said, "Nothing you can blame on the ranchers, Wade. Every man has to look out for himself."

"Just what I'm saying; there ain't no teamwork. But that's neither here nor yonder. It's happening, and we've got to have help. That's why we sent for you, Jim."

Holt's brows lifted. "We? That mean all the ranchers are in on this?"

"Every last one. Me, Bevan, Johnson, Damion King, Dutch Kastner—the whole Basin. We all got the same trouble, the same problem."

"And what's that?"

"Rustling. Tearing down corrals and holding pens. Burning line shacks and barns. Range fires. You name about any kind of cussedness and we've got it."

"Sounds like homesteaders again."

Bevan shook his head. "Not that. Ain't a one left in the Basin. My hunch is that it's a regular, organized bunch of rustlers."

"Organized is sure the word," McClendon muttered.

"They got things figured down to a fine point. Set fire to a man's hay barn or line shack, or maybe a section of his land; then while he's busy with his crew fighting the flames, they skip off with thirty, forty head of beef."

"Shouldn't be any trouble tracking a herd that size," Jim said.

"Seems so, but we ain't never been able to. They got a cute trick of wiping out their tracks by running other steers over their trail."

Holt shrugged. "They've got to go somewhere," he said, twirling his empty glass between his palms. Lifting his eyes to Cully, he said, "Funny you or some of your crew hasn't spotted them being moved out."

The foreman's swollen face reddened and his eyes once more glowed with anger. "Usually happens at night. And like Mr. McClendon says, there's always something going on, keeping us busy. Last time there was a stampede—"

"Cully's doing his best," McClendon broke in. "But he's got a fair-sized job of his own to look after. I'm running near four thousand head right now. Puts all his time into looking after them."

Holt shifted his attention to Bevan. "That pretty much the way it is with you and the rest of the ranchers?"

"Just the same."

"And nobody's got any idea what happens to the steers after they're rustled. They just drop out of sight."

"About the size of it," Bevan said. "Sure costing us a

pretty penny. It keeps on, we're going to lose what we've gained in the past few years."

"They're even driving off calves," McClendon said. "Tally this year's away below normal—and there ain't no other reason why the drop would be less. Just getting stole before we ever put an iron on them."

"Rustlers don't usually fool with calves," Jim said thoughtfully. "Not worth trailing to market."

"They don't unless somebody's building a herd," Bevan commented. "And that's what I figure's going on. Be easy to load a bunch on a wagon, haul them off."

"Be wheel tracks—"

"Wagon could be stashed somewheres outside the Basin, in that rough country west of here maybe."

"Anybody ever ride over there for a look?"

McClendon glanced at Cully Ryan. The foreman nodded. "Sure we've done some looking. Ain't no place a man could go over there. Nothing but rocks and arroyos that lead up to them bluffs at the foot of the mountains. Even a man on foot can't climb them."

McClendon rubbed at his jaw, turned to Bevan. "How about your crew? They done any searching out in them roughs this side of the mountain?"

"Some, but like Cully says, it's a waste of time. Nobody could drive stock through there. Besides, where'd they go? Ain't nothing but flats on the other side of the mountain running all the way from hell to hallelujah. Not a town for two hundred miles—and no water!"

"If they got through, they could head south for a

ways, then swing east," Holt pointed out.

"That's the whole point!" Bevan said. "They just couldn't get through. There ain't no trail. . . . Anyway, we all got ideas who it is."

Jim Holt turned to McClendon, surprise blanking his features. "Then why—"

"Ideas, that's all we got. Me—I ain't so sure as some of the others."

"You mean it's somebody here in the Basin?"

"Not exactly here. Out on the edge," Bevan said. "The old Oatman place. He sold out. Reckon you didn't know that."

"Saw he had an office in town. Real estate and such, the sign said."

"Moved off the place a couple years back. Never did much good there himself."

"Who bought it?"

"Three men. Ex-cons, the lot of them. I figure they're just setting up there getting fat off our herds."

"You keep an eye on them?"

"Sure. We've took turns putting men to watching the place. Too smart for us. Never been able to catch them red-handed at anything."

"Your trouble start about the same time they took over Oatman's?"

McClendon bobbed his head. "Did, all right. That's what makes Jack and the others think Bogard and them two with him are at the bottom of it."

Holt straightened slowly. "Who?"

"Jasper by the name of Bogard. Dave Bogard. Served time for a holdup. Stagecoach, I think it was.

Ones with him are Ivan Wright and a Mex *vaquero* named Delgado."

"Was I laying odds," Cully Ryan said, leaning back in his chair, "I'd say that's where the rustling's coming from whether we got proof or not."

"Well, I ain't condemning no man unless that *is* what I got," McClendon said.

Holt, his eyes on Ryan, shifted his attention to the rancher.

"Anybody ever talk to Bogard about it?"

McClendon shrugged. "Well, you don't just walk up to a man and ask him if he's stealing your cattle; but I rode by there one day. Mentioned I was missing some stock and wondered if he'd seen any drifting around. Told me no. Was plenty cool about it."

"Then was I laying odds," Holt said, mimicking Cully Ryan, "I'd say he was telling you straight. Dave Bogard's not a liar."

❊ IV ❊

IN THE QUIET that fell abruptly over the room, the rattle of pans and clinking of dishes in the kitchen where Martha McClendon was preparing the evening meal was loud. Bevan finally broke the hush.

"You know this here Bogard?"

Jim nodded. "Knew him before he was sent to the pen in Santa Fe. I've seen him a few times since he got out. Told me he was going to settle down, that he was done with outlawing. I believe him."

Bevan turned slowly to McClendon. "I'm wondering

maybe if you've—if we—sent for the wrong man to handle this. . . . Being a friend of his—"

The rancher's gaze was on the floor. His face was in a deep frown and beads of sweat stood out on his forehead. His shoulders stirred.

"Think I know Jim Holt well enough to know it won't make any difference—them being friends, I mean. If he finds Bogard's at the bottom of the rustling, he'll still do what's right, what we're expecting him to do." McClendon raised his eyes to Holt. "That the way it'll be?"

"That's the way it'll be," Jim said. "Only I'll tell you now, you're wrong. Dave's a lot of things but he's not a liar. When he told me he aimed to keep his nose clean, I figure he meant it."

"How about the others? You know them, too?"

"Names are not familiar. Might, once I get a look at them."

"Seems you're mighty sure of this Bogard," Ryan said. "You ever run together?"

"Nope. Once got myself in a tight, however. Dave stepped in, gave me a hand."

"So you feel you owe him a favor," Bevan said with a gusty sigh. "Reckon that tears it, Wade. This fellow'll be about as much use to us as ticks on a heifer."

"What's between Bogard and me won't count here," Jim said quietly. "You hire me to do a job, I'll do it."

"But you don't aim to do much looking far as these convicts are concerned, I expect," Ryan said.

"Matter of fact, I will. Don't expect to find anything unless maybe some information that could put me on the right track."

"It's got to be them!" Bevan said suddenly. "Everything points that way."

"Only thing I see making you feel that way is that they've been in the pen. Nothing says a man can't go straight when he gets out."

"Odds are against it. Besides, like we told you, this trouble didn't begin until after they'd moved in."

"Still no proof they're the ones."

Bevan came to his feet in a sudden lurch, hands spread wide. "You see?" he shouted, facing McClendon. "He's got his mind made up. We can't expect him to do anything, not with them being his friends. Hell, we're wasting time and money hiring him—"

"Now, hold on, Jack—"

"I know he's a man who can handle the job. You don't have to keep telling me that. I remember what he done here five years ago. But this is something else. We've got a situation here where his friends are the guilty ones and we can't look for him to go digging up proof that'll put them at the end of a rope, 'specially since he figures he owes one of them a favor."

McClendon rose to his feet then, motioned Bevan to be seated. "Just calm down, Jack. Ain't nothing gained by jumping up and ranting around. I'll admit I never expected something like this, but I ain't so sure it changes the picture none."

"It doesn't," Holt said. "You want me to break up the rustling that's going on. I'll do it. But if it'll make you all feel better about it, I'll pass the chore, ride on, and you can bring in somebody else."

"What we'd better do," Cully Ryan said. "Been too much stock lost already, and if we go making a mistake—"

"Seems to me," Holt cut in coldly, "being ramrod of this ranch you could've done a little more of a job looking after McClendon's stock. What you're paid for."

Ryan's color deepened. He pushed forward on his chair. "You hinting that maybe I've got something to do with what's been going on?"

"Not unless you want to take it that way, but handling rustlers is part of a foreman's job. McClendon said you'd been busy with the herds—sort of covering up for you. It's some of those herds you're so busy looking after that's being rustled."

"Never mind," McClendon said wearily. "What's done is done and there ain't nothing any of us can do to change that. Problem is to get it stopped. Jim, I'm asking you straight out—you think you can do it?"

"I'm willing to try."

"Trying don't mean doing," Bevan said drily. "We need a better answer than that. What if it turns out your friend Bogard and his sidekicks are the rustlers that everybody in the Jicarilla Basin thinks they are. You going to look the other way or will you bring them in?"

"They'll be brought in if I'm convinced they're the ones I'm hunting for."

"That's good enough for me," Wade McClendon said with finality. "Jim, you got yourself—"

"May not be good enough for Johnson, King, and the

others," Bevans interrupted. "Not when they hear all the facts."

"Well, I'll guarantee it," McClendon said heatedly. "You tell that to them, Jack, when you start passing the word along."

Bevan looked closely at the rancher. "Sort of crawling out on a limb, ain't you?"

"Maybe I am, but I don't think so. I'll personally stand behind Jim Holt seven days a week, and I'll be right."

"I'm hoping so," Bevan muttered, giving in. "This thing's gone too far now. We should've called in somebody a long time ago."

"Brings up something I've had in the back of my mind," McClendon said. "Jim mentioned it, too. Maybe we ought to have a good lawman around, way things've changed. When he gets this rustling cleaned up, you be in favor of giving him the job as marshal? He'll sure as hell have earned—"

"You won't owe me anything except the money you'll pay me for running down your rustlers."

"But being town marshal. . . . A steady job. . . ."

"Obliged, but no thanks. Hard enough to please one man, much less a whole town—and a bunch of ranchers."

"Well, it's up to you. If you change your mind—"

"I won't. Now, about what I came here for, you want me to take on the job?"

"Of course we do!"

"Then let's get the cards out on the table. It'll have to be my way—nobody interfering. I'm to have free rein, go and come as I please and no questions asked. I call on anybody handy when and if I need help. That understood?"

McClendon nodded. "Cully'll work with you whenever you say. So will the rest of my crew. Same goes for every rancher in the Basin."

"I don't want anybody taking off on their own; I want it all left to me. Somebody second-guessing me always makes me nervous."

"Won't nobody try it. Ain't that right, Jack?"

Bevan shrugged. "Don't see as we've got much of a choice."

McClendon gave the rancher an angry look, swung to Ryan. "You got it all clear, too, Cully?"

The Circle X foreman nodded slowly. "Whatever you say, Mr. McClendon."

"Then it's all set. Jack, I'll leave it to you to pass the word up the Basin to the other ranchers. Jim'll be headquartering out of here. Of course he'll be circulating around, but if anybody wants him, they can come here, leave word. I've got a spare room—"

Holt waved aside. "Like staying in the bunkhouse better. And taking my meals there, too. Easier to move around."

"Suit yourself. Cully'll have a bunk for you," the rancher said and, as his foreman came to his feet, added, "See that he's taken care of."

Ryan bobbed his head, turned for the door. Bevan swung in behind him, and then as Holt started to follow, McClendon dropped a hand on his shoulder.

"Hold on now, Jim. You can start your eating with

30

the crew in the morning. Tonight you're having supper with me and the missus. Been looking forward to hashing over old times with you."

❈ V ❈

I T WAS well after dark when Jim Holt finally was able to break away from McClendon and make his way to the bunkhouse. The rancher had tried again to persuade him to stay in the main house, use the spare bedroom that was available, but Jim refused. The offer was tempting and the obvious comforts were not to be considered lightly, but he felt the closer he was to the men who rode the hills and flats day in and day out, the better his chances of turning up the guilty parties.

Not that he suspected anyone in particular; in truth, everyone including Wade McClendon himself—as ridiculous as that might seem—was suspect. Jim Holt had been around long enough, and through plenty of similar situations, to know that an open mind was the only trail to a solution of the puzzle.

Light still shown in the bunkhouse windows, and he could hear the drone of conversation as he walked up two steps to the landing and reached for the screen door knob.

Instantly all talk ceased, and as he entered the long room lined on either side with bunks, he felt the eyes of a dozen men swing to him, hang there, give him their frank appraisal.

Only the face of Cully Ryan was familiar. The others he'd met—Reno, Billy Jay and Earl Munger—were not present, evidently working night watch on the range. That followed, as they had been in town with Ryan during the day. There was also the possibility that the three men were special friends of the Circle X foreman—more or less came and went as they pleased. . . . That was something he'd look into.

Holt laid his questioning glance on Ryan who pointed indifferently at a bunk at the end of the row. It was in a corner some distance from any window where relief from the heat might be found.

Jim nodded, walked the length of the row, halted. The beds this side and adjacent to one of the windows appeared not to be in use. He swung his attention to the foreman.

"How about one of these?"

Ryan shrugged. "Suit yourself. I figured you being a big, high-faluting rustler-catcher, you'd sort of want to be by yourself and not associate with us common cowhands."

Holt favored Cully with a humorless grin. "Something in what you say," he replied, "but I like breathing. I'll take this one."

Hanging his saddlebags on the peg, and dropping his blanket roll onto the slatted bunk, he sat down, faced the room. Ryan had not stirred, continued to stare at him with unblinding, sullen eyes.

"Something bothering you?"

Cully spat. "Didn't much like some of the things you said. You trying to make it look like I'm not doing my job?"

"Are you?" Holt asked softly.

"You're goddamn right I am! Ain't nobody puts in the time I do around this place. Nobody!"

"But you've never seen any signs of rustling. . . ."

"That don't mean nothing! Nobody else has either."

"Somebody has," Jim said, shaking his head. "Can't tell me there's fifteen men working the range day and night and none of them never spotted something that didn't look right. Makes no sense."

"Sense or not, that's the way of it; and it sure ain't going to be healthy for you around here if you go running loose, accusing everybody—"

"Not accusing anybody—*yet*. But I reckon it won't take long."

Ryan came angrily to his feet. Leveling a finger at Holt, he said, "Well, I'm giving you a warning right now. Stay off my back! I'm not standing for you riding me none, not when it's plain who's at the bottom of all this rustling and burning—"

"You don't know anything, you just think you do."

"The hell! Everybody knows it's them jailbirds up on the Oatman place, only I don't expect you to see it that way—not when you're a *compadre* of theirs."

Jim Holt pulled himself upright. In the shadowy, lamplit room he appeared even larger. "If you've got anything for certain I can go on, spit it out. Far as Bogard and the other two men are concerned, they'll get the same treatment as anybody else. Now, if you know something, let's hear it."

Ryan's gaze dropped, touched the intent faces of the men around him. "I got nothing for sure. It's only—"

"Then keep your mouth shut. Talk like that's what

gets lynching parties started."

An elderly puncher about midway down the row, raised his head and propped it on a bent arm. "It true them jailbirds are good friends of your'n?"

"I know one—Dave Bogard."

"You owing him some kind of a favor?"

"My life. Any time a man does that for you I guess you could say you owe him."

The old rider grunted, settled back. "Yeh, you sure do. Only. . . ."

"Only what?"

"Only there ain't none of us can see how you'll ever get much done far as they're concerned," Ryan finished, "you feeling the way you do about them."

"Don't lose no sleep over it!" Holt snapped. "Now, is there anything else sticking in your craw? Let's get it out in the open. I aim to go to work in the morning and I don't want you grumping around like an old woman. Goes for every man in this room."

Silence followed. Several of the men lay back on their bunks, turned away. Cully Ryan shrugged.

"I'll be doing my job," he said. "Let's see if you'll be doing yours."

"Good enough," Jim said and crawled into his own bed. But he knew the matter would not end there. In spite of Wade McClendon's orders, he'd get little help from Cully Ryan and the other crew members; he'd find only hostility.

It WENT further than that, Holt discovered, that next morning when he rode north from Circle X and pulled into Bevan's yard. The rancher, accompanied by Carl Johnson and Damion King, came out onto the porch immediately when he drew up to the hitchrack.

Bevan had already briefed them on the situation, he saw, and was aware also of their frank skepticism and disapproval. It was evident on their scowling faces. They, too, were convinced that Dave Bogard and his friends were responsible for the trouble in the Basin and felt that he would do little, if anything, about putting a stop to their activities.

Staying on the saddle, the nodded to the ranchers, "Good to see you again Carl, Damion."

The two men returned his greeting with only a slight inclination of their heads. Johnson reached into his pocket for a cigar, bit off the end, searched for a match.

"Bogard's place is the other direction," he said pointedly.

"Know that," Jim answered evenly. "Few things I'd like to know, however."

"Seems to me you already know everything that's necessary to haul down those outlaws."

"Meaning the fact that they were once in the pen?"

"Ain't that enough?" Damion King demanded hotly.

"Not hardly. You want to answer a few questions, or have you got your minds so made up you won't talk?"

Johnson spat, glanced at King and Jack Bevan. "What kind of questions?"

"About the stock you've lost. There any particular pattern in the way it's been done?"

"Pattern?"

"I mean—is it always at night? Does it always

happen when something else is going on—like a fire maybe?"

King, a portly, red-faced man, rubbed at his jowls. "Well, come to think of it, always is at night near as I can tell. And usually something's going on, like that fire at Dutch's. Lost forty head that night."

"But you can't be sure it's always at night," Johnson said. "You find out about it in the day. You just figure the rustling took place at night."

"What I'm trying to pin down," Holt said. "Sort of got the same idea from McClendon. How about the stock? Is it usually steers grazing close to the mountains, or have they run off stuff from 'most all parts of the range?"

Bevan looked faintly surprised, "Come to think of it, beef I've lost has been what I was running on the open range." He turned to Johnson and King. "It the same with you?"

Both men nodded. King said, "Never gave it no thought, but I guess that's right. Why? What help's that?"

"Means the rustlers pick stock that's close to brush country—stuff they can drive off quick before anybody spots them."

Johnson wagged his head. "Won't hold water. We've gone looking for tracks but never found none."

"McClendon told me tracks were usually wiped out by running other cattle over them."

"Well, yeh, guess that's the way it's been now that I—"

"Means Bogard and his bunch are plenty smart,"

Jack Bevan said. "They grab only a piece of a herd, use the rest to cover up what they've done. Anyway, with all the stock grazing out there, you'll find tracks all over the place."

"Which brings up something I've been harping on all along," Holt said. "Riders driving cattle across the range would be seen by somebody, yet nobody ever has seen anything."

"Sure is kind of funny," Johnson admitted. "And I don't see how anybody ever could drive stock into the mountains. No trail and hardly nothing but solid rock all the way west of the Basin. Cattle couldn't walk on that."

"So we come right back to Bogard," Bevan said. "He's the only answer."

"Not until we've got some proof."

"And that's something that's set us to wondering," Damion King said. "If you find it, and it points to Bogard, will you speak up?"

"What I've been hired to do," Holt said coldly. "No matter who it is—you, some of the hired hands, McClendon, or anybody else in the Basin—you'll know about it."

King's face was taut. "You saying maybe it's one of us?"

"Only making it clear that whoever it is, he'll be brought in," Holt said and wheeled away.

He was growing a little weary of reassuring the ranchers that he would do the job he'd assumed, and was impatient with their closed mind attitude toward Dave Bogard and his two friends. Johnson called something after him but he gave it no attention, simply rode on, heading straight out across the Basin for the far side of the open range area.

He had learned nothing of particular value from the ranchers, he realized; the rustling could be taking place at night, but as one of them had mentioned, the loss was never noted except during the day. The cattle could have been stolen in the early morning, late afternoon, or even a day previous. And there were never any signs left, never any trace.

That was what puzzled Jim Holt most, and a considerable time later after he had crossed the range and reached the brushy, rock-studded area that marked the western fringe of the Basin, he pulled the sorrel to a halt and thoughtfully considered the ragged country extending on to the towering mountains in the distance.

It seemed unlikely that a herd, however small, could be driven through such a wild and broken land. There appeared to be nothing but a maze of deep arroyos, brush, scattered boulders, rocky benches and canyons running to all directions, terminating finally at the jagged palisades forming the face of the mountain itself. And, as someone had pointed out, if the rustlers did drive stock into that hell-hole area, where would they take them?

But it was something he'd have to look into. There had to be an answer, and all things considered, it probably lay in the badlands. He'd have himself a little trip into the area, he decided.

First, though, he wanted to see Dave Bogard, meet

him and the men with him. He wanted to hear Bogard tell him in so many words that he had nothing to do with the rustling that was going on in the Basin.

❈ VI ❈

THERE HAD BEEN no improvements made on the Oatman property. That was quickly apparent to Jim Holt when, late in the afternoon, he climbed out of the Basin onto the plateau where the ranch lay. The same weathered, square-shaped house, three or four equally shabby outbuildings, several corrals, all baking in the sunlight without benefit of trees or shrubbery of any kind.

Reece Oatman, when he owned the place, had done nothing for it, simply getting by with the barest of necessities. It appeared Dave Bogard was following his example, accomplishing even less along those lines, if such was possible.

A vague uneasiness stirred through Jim Holt. Men endeavoring to build a ranch, make something for themselves, would spend their spare time on the property repairing, replacing the outworn, perhaps improving and enlarging to some extent.

There was no indication of such here; only a definite lack of interest. Could that mean that Bogard and the men with him did not intend to make a going concern of the Oatman ranch? That they wanted it only as a place at which to headquarter and serve as a blind for other activities?

It was a disturbing thought and the possibility of it

being true was much too great. But Dave Bogard had told him—sworn, actually—that he was going straight, that he never again wanted to see the inside of a jail much less the high walls of a penitentiary. Dave Bogard had never lied to him before; not even the time when to avoid the truth would have permitted him to go free.

But a man can change, and now Jim Holt was having doubts concerning his friend. Everything he'd heard seemed to point to the three ex-convicts, and a glimpse of the so-called ranch tended to strengthen what he had been told.

Still, there was no real proof. To go on the appearance of the ranch was as stupid as blaming the rustling on the men simply because they once had been outlaws. The two men with Dave—Wright and a Mexican named Delgado—maybe that was the answer. Maybe they were carrying on a side business of cattle thievery unbeknown to Bogard, doublecrossing him in effect. But that possibility tumbled of its own weight; Dave Bogard was no fool. He'd know if such was going on.

Halting at the edge of the clearing, Jim Holt studied the sagging house and outbuildings in moody silence. There appeared to be no one around. He could see three or four horses in a corral next to the small barn, but they likely were extra mounts. Chances were the three men were out on the range somewhere. They should be coming in shortly for their evening meal, however. That is, under normal ranching schedule they would; if they were engaging in activities other than—

Holt felt that nagging worry fade as three riders

broke over a rise a hundred yards below the house, ride forward slowly, and pull to a stop at the corral directly behind the house.

Dave Bogard, his reddish beard glinting in the lowering sun, dismounted stiffly, dragged off his battered hat, and mopped his balding head. He looked much the same as he did years ago. Wright was a lean, older man with a narrow face and small, close-set eyes. Delgado, the *vaquero,* seemed much younger and showed it in the smooth, easy grace of his movements.

"I take the horses," he said, gathering the reins. There was an affection in the softness of his voice and manner, almost as if he were the son looking after well-loved parents.

"Might as well leave that bonebag of mine here," Wright said. "Be using him again after we grub down."

"A job I can do for you, *viejo,*" Delgado said.

Wright's head came up sharply. "Reckon I can still pull my own weight around here, *amigo!*"

Delgado smiled, nodded, and led the horses into the corral. Bogard wheeled, entered the house, followed by the older man. The *vaquero* fooled around with his charge for a few minutes, slackening off the gear, kicking a pile of hay toward each. Then he, too, crossed the narrow yard and disappeared into the shack.

Holt waited out another full minute, and then moving out from the fringe of rabbitbush into the open, called, "Hello—the house!"

The *vaquero* appeared instantly, a tense, coiled figure, features dark, hands hanging at his sides. The colors of his ordinarily gaudy clothing, stripped of their silver ornamentations appeared drab in the driving sunlight. Only his big Mexican spurs showed bright.

Bogard appeared next, and Wright, a rifle cradled on his arms, followed. All three men watched as Holt rode in slowly, and then suddenly Bogard threw up his hands, stepped forward.

"Jim! What the hell you doing out this way? Last time I seen you was in Abilene more'n a year ago!" Abruptly he halted, looked back to the waiting men. "He's a friend of mine, boys. Plenty all right."

Holt stopped at the hitchrack, swung down. He stepped from behind the sorrel to meet Bogard, hand extended, approaching.

"Good to see you again, Dave," he said as he took the man's fingers into his own. Pausing, he glanced to the others.

Hurriedly Bogard said, "Want you to meet my partners, Jim. That young squirt there's Nestor Delgado. We call him Del, for short."

The *vaquero* stepped up, nodded gravely and shook hands, his eyes saying nothing.

"The other'n is Ivan Wright . . . maybe you two've already met—"

"Can't say as we have," Holt said, shaking with the older man. Wright, like Delgado, merely nodded and moved back, waited in the way of men unsure—neither accepting nor rejecting a new acquaintance.

"Hear you've got yourself in the cattle business," Holt said, glancing around.

"For a fact," Bogard replied, "but I ain't in it much. Not yet, anyways. How about eating with us? Was just getting ready. It'll be beans, biscuits and venison wet down with chicory—"

"Suits me fine if I'm not horning in."

"Horning in!" Bogard echoed, throwing a quick glance at Wright and the *vaquero*. "This here oversized galoot is probably the best friend I ever had! No, sir, you ain't horning in, Jim! Come on, let's go inside."

Ivan Wright apparently took care of the cooking chores. He went immediately to the stove, got a fire going, and then began to put the meal together. Bogard shoved a chair at Jim. "Make yourself comfortable for a bit," and reaching for several tin plates and a handful of knives and forks, he dropped them onto the table.

"It ain't much," Bogard said, glancing around the small room, "but it's a start—for all of us."

"Once had some thoughts about buying this place myself," Holt said.

Dave Bogard paused. "You been around these parts before?"

"Five years back I worked for McClendon, the Circle X outfit down in the Basin. Man by the name of Oatman was here then."

"That's who I bought it from. Two hundred dollars cash money down, two hundred dollars a year for the next three. I don't meet the payment I lose the whole shebang."

"Not a bad price. Could be turned into a pretty fair little spread."

"What we're hoping to do with it. Ivan and Del are

pitching in with me. Aim to do some fixing up, but it takes time and cash. . . . You working for McClendon again?"

"Him—and the rest of the ranchers in the Basin."

Ivan Wright came around slowly. Delgado appeared in the doorway of the adjoining room where sleeping quarters were maintained. Even Bogard's features hardened.

"Reckon that means you're up here to see if we've got anything to do with the rustling that's going on."

Holt nodded, making no bones about it. Wright swore, slammed the piece of wood he was holding into the firebox.

"Goddammit! Can't they leave us be?" he shouted. "We ain't rustled no cows—and don't aim to. What we got we bought, and if you're a poking around here, trying to pin something on us—"

"Came up here mostly to say hello to Dave, meet you and Del," Holt said quietly.

"But I'm betting you're wondering—maybe even figuring—the same as them ranchers and them counterjumpers in town do."

"No, seems I'm about the only man around who doesn't. They gave me that kind of talk and I told them they were wrong, that Dave Bogard had promised me he was going straight and he wasn't a liar."

Bogard's head dropped. "Obliged to you for that, Jim. You always was one for standing by a man. I don't guess they took much stock in what you said, however."

"They've all got their minds pretty well made up."

44

"Well, we ain't mixed up in no rustling, or anything like that at all. You've got my word on it. And Ivan and Del's in the same pot as me. Ain't none of us wants to get crossways with the law again."

Wright resumed his preparation of the meal. From the doorway, the *vaquero* said, "It is hard to live, *señor.* Nobody forgets we were once in the penitentiary. It is like the bite of a wolf—a man always has the scar."

"Folks are like that," Holt said. "And they'll have to be shown, have to have things proved to them. Even then, there's some who won't ever let you forget it. Just something you'd best figure on living with."

Bogard slumped onto one of the chairs. His ruddy face was sober. "How bad's the feeling, Jim? They really set on the idea that it's us doing the rustling?"

"Got nobody else they can blame it on. And you three are good bets, they figure."

"But they've got nothing to make them think—no proof, I mean—"

"That's what's held them back—that and McClendon. He's square and he's bull headed. Not the kind to go flying off half-cocked. But things are getting pretty hot. Reason he sent for me. I'm to run down whoever's doing it. You got any ideas?"

Wright turned from his stove again. "That mean you ain't got your mind made up that it's us?"

"Thought I'd made that clear already. Did hope you might have some ideas—a hunch, maybe. Or you could have seen riders."

Wright grunted, resumed his chores. Bogard said, "We stick pretty close to the place. Going to try building a new house soon's as we get time. Need a barn that don't leak like a sieve, too. Between watching the herd and falling timber, we don't range far. . . . Can't say as I've ever even seen dust hanging around."

"Me neither," Ivan Wright said in a more amiable tone.

"You lost any stock?"

"None," Bogard said, and then added, "Reckon that don't sound so good. A rustler sure wouldn't steal his own beef. But fact is we only got around forty head and they're pastured just a short ways west of the house. No job for three growed men to look after forty steers. They come with the place."

"I can see it," Jim said. "But some of the ranchers in the Basin will think it's funny your herd's never raided."

"The hell with them!" Wright snapped. "Ain't no way on God's green earth for us to get along with them or anybody else. They won't believe nothing good about us because they plain don't want to!

"Now, if you want to go out look the place over, comb it right good for rustled stock; you're welcome to do it because you're a friend of Dave's. But that don't go for any of them! First one ever to set foot on this place is asking for a rifle bullet."

"No need for that happening," Holt said. "I take your word and they've got to take mine. All I'm asking for is help. Keep your eyes peeled. You see anything that doesn't look right, get word to me at McClendon's quick. Now, let's forget it. That cooking of yours smells mighty good. We about ready to try it?"

Ivan Wright stared, and then his weathered, old face crinkled into a grin. "Sure thing, about ready, Jim. Just you make yourself comfortable for a couple more minutes."

❊ VII ❊

THERE WAS a weak moon, and aided by the stars, it laid a pale, silver glow over the land as Jim Holt rode slowly across the range on his way home. Coyotes barked in the rocky fastness to the west, and now and then an owl hooted a forlorn question and doves cried of their loneliness.

Dave Bogard and his friends had nothing to do with the rustling that was taking place in the Basin. He was convinced of that now. There had been no doubt in his mind insofar as Bogard himself was concerned from the start, but he had wondered about the men with him.

Now he was sure of them also. Ivan Wright and the *vaquero* felt exactly as did Bogard; anything, however disagreeable, was preferable to a life behind bars, and none of them would risk anything that might return them to a cell.

"Just plain starving's better," Wright had declared as they sat on the stoop outside the shack drinking coffee. "But we ain't going to come to that; not with deer running around everywhere loose, same as are rabbits and quail."

"Ivan figures to put us in a garden next spring," Dave had said then. "Corn, cabbage and the like. He got to be quite a farmer when he was serving time. Was head gardner at the pen."

"Aimed to do it this spring," Wright had added. "Just weren't no time, and no spare cash for seed neither. Next year'll be different, howsomever."

"You going to sell some stock?" Jim asked.

"Ain't done it so far. Been hanging onto everything. But we figure we can spare ten or fifteen head next summer. Give us enough money to do some things that need doing."

They'd make a go of the place, Holt felt, if they were left alone, allowed to work and build as they planned. And that was the way it would be if he had anything to say about it. Best way to help was to run down the outlaws, stop the trouble that was stirring up the Basin. Then there would be no reason for the ranchers to think—

The dark shape of a rider flashed across Jim Holt's vision a hundred yards ahead in the grove through which he was passing.

He jerked the sorrel to a halt instinctively, and then as realization came to him, he leaned forward, dug spurs into the gelding and gave chase. Maybe—by a streak of good luck—he'd stumbled onto the rustlers!

The big, red horse leaped forward, began to weave in and out of the trees, following the natural aisles all dappled with moonlight. A short time later, Jim saw the rider again—hunched low over the saddle, riding hard for a line of squat bluffs at the end of the grove.

He could tell nothing about the man or the horse because of the half darkness. It could be anyone. But he was closing the gap that separated them. Once out of the trees and on the flat that fronted the bluffs, the sorrel's great speed would overhaul the rider's mount quickly.

Suddenly the night echoed with a gunshot. Jim heard the bullet clip through the brush close by. Another blast ripped the darkness. Instantly Holt swerved to one side. The sorrel stumbled as the rifle cracked again, but the gelding was unhurt, had only caught a hoof against an exposed root—a near accident that probably saved Holt from being hit.

The shooting was coming from the end of the bluffs directly ahead. The powder flash of the last shot had been clear. Veering the sorrel again to avoid any pattern, Jim hauled up in a dense thicket of mountain mahogany and leaped from the saddle. Pistol in hand, he crouched low. Then he circled the brush, came in on the bluffs from their lower end.

The bushwhacker had hidden himself there, Holt was certain. If he swung a bit wide, worked his way up from the rear, he could take the man by surprise.

Ducking low again, he doubled back, circled, came in a second time now more to the east end of the ragged formations. Halting long enough to catch his breath, he eased forward, careful of each footstep and making use of every bit of cover.

He stopped at the foot of the bluff. The hidden rifleman should be directly in front of him on the opposite side of the butte. Crouched in the blackness behind a clump of sage, he debated the wisdom of climbing the formation with the chance that his approach might be heard, or of moving along its base—a quieter route but not so advantageous. He decided on the latter.

Hunched low, Jim moved out of the brush, picking his way carefully and quietly, keeping as close to the foot of the bluff as possible. His nerves were taut and sweat clothed his face, misted his eyes. He paused, brushed his forehead impatiently, resumed the tense stalk.

Again he halted. Someone or something had stirred. The noise came from ahead and slightly above him. He waited out a long minute, heard no more, resumed his approach.

A brilliant flash blinded him. Burning particles of gun-powder slapped at his face and neck. His hat was swept from his head in a mighty rush of wind and sound. He stumbled backwards, tripped, fell hard. His head struck something solid and for a moment his senses reeled.

And then he was rolling away, seeking safety in the shadows of nearby brush. Reaching cover, he came to his knees, pistol leveled while he sought to focus his stinging eyes, locate the bushwhacker somewhere on the slope.

The quick pounding of hooves racketed through the night's hush. Holt swore feelingly, came upright and ran forward to the edge of the grade. The rider was disappearing into a band of trees at the far end of the bluffs. Jim stood for a time staring into the darkness where the rifleman had vanished, and then moving on up the slope, searched about until he located the brushy pocket behind a flat ledge where the bushwhacker had hidden.

Three brass cartridge casings lay where they had fallen when ejected. He picked them up, and crouched behind the shelf, he struck a match and examined the slim cylinders. . . . They meant nothing, were of no help at all. Of the common, everyday type and caliber, he could probably find a rifle to fit them on half the saddles in the Basin.

Stuffing them into his pocket, he recovered his hat and hurried to the sorrel. Mounting, he struck for McClendon's at a fast gallop. There was a chance that, if the two riders—and there had been two; one who led him into the ambush, and one who waited with a rifle—worked for Circle X, he could yet discover who they were.

He came into the yard at Circle X in a rush, drew up at the corral where the crew had loosed their mounts. Leaving the saddle, he climbed the poles, dropped to the ground and passed hurriedly among the horses, laying a hand on each. All were cool, had not been ridden for hours.

Anger still pushing him, he crossed to the barn, checked the animals there with the same result. Half a dozen horses were in a corral south of that building. He examined them, did no better.

Returning to the hardpack, he halted in a pool of blackness behind a small shed to think. The bushwhackers, if they were Circle X men and had returned to the ranch after making their attempt on his life, could have anticipated his move and picketed their mounts in the brush where he would not find them. If so, there was no point in further searching.

Too, assuming the pair had been McClendon men, there was the possibility they were among the punchers who were doing nighthawk duty on the range, and would not have returned to the ranch at all. They would not be expected until the day crew relieved them in the morning.

Why had he concluded the bushwhackers were Circle X riders?

That question posed itself as he moved on to where the sorrel waited. He thought about it while he stripped his gear and turned the gelding into the corral. There was no solid basis for the assumption; it had just lodged in his mind somehow. Perhaps it was because he had been on McClendon range when the attempt was made.

But that proved nothing, he realized as he headed for the bunkhouse, just as finding no still-warm horses on the premises proved nothing. However—he came to a halt just inside the dimly lit bunkhouse—there was a chance he could learn something.

Pulling off his boots, he started down the rows of bunks, glancing at each, trying to remember which had been occupied and which had been vacant. All seemed as it had been the night previous except for Cully Ryan's bed. It had not been used.

"Who you looking for?" a sleepy voice came from across the aisle.

Jim turned to the puncher. "Cully."

"Went to town," the man said, rolling over. "Some gal he's sparking, heard the cook say."

Maybe, Holt thought and moved on to his bunk. One thing was sure; he'd stirred up a worry in somebody.

❊ VIII ❊

THE DAY CREW had eaten and ridden out and the night shift was already in when Jim Holt came into breakfast that next morning. Under the sullen glances of Joe Reno, Billy Jay, Munger— and several others—he found a place at the long table and began his meal, wondering if the pair who had attempted the ambush were perhaps within arm's reach.

Helping himself from the platter piled high with fried bacon and potatoes, he leaned back to wait while the cook filled his coffee cup, and then began to eat, fully aware of the curious as well as suspicious looks being cast at him by the punchers ranged along the table.

He had considered mentioning the incident and watching sharply for any reactions that might lead to the identities of the bushwhackers, but brushed it aside. He would be unable to prove anything. Better to keep whoever it was guessing, not let on that he had any idea who the pair were—which, in truth, he didn't.

And he'd not report it to Wade McClendon, either. The rancher would probably conclude that Bogard and his partners were responsible since he had been coming from their ranch, and fearing their activities were about to be uncovered, had hurriedly ridden out to head off that danger. It would be a logical chain of thought, one to which all of the ranchers would subscribe.

But it hadn't been Dave Bogard. Nor had it been Ivan Wright or the *vaquero*. Jim Holt would bet his life on that. They had too much to lose, and besides, their word counted with him, just as his did with them.

Best just to keep his mouth shut about the incident, go an about the business of ferreting out the real outlaws. He had them worried now, and something was bound to turn up; somebody would make a slip and put him on the right track. . . . Maybe someone in town—the old marshal, Pete Hornbuckle—might know something that would help.

No one took the lawman seriously; and for that very reason he could have some knowledge that in itself meant nothing, but fitted into the overall puzzle, could have value. He'd ride into Butte, exchange a few words with Pete, and maybe hang around the saloon a bit. It was surprising what a man could learn in a place like a saloon.

He found Hornbuckle in his dusty office, slumped in a chair, feet propped on the desk. The two cells were empty, appeared to have had no occupants for some time. As he halted in the doorway, the marshal gave him a surprised glance and then smiled.

"Was wondering if I was going to see you again."

Holt's interest picked up instantly. "Something make you think you wouldn't?"

Hornbuckle's feet dropped to the floor with a thud. He yawned, pointed to one of the chairs. "Come in and set a spell. No, nothing special 'cepting I learned who you are, that McClendon and the others brought you in here to clean up the Basin. Some of the folks are betting you won't be around for long. . . . Ain't like it was five years ago, they say."

"Who're saying that?"

"Nobody much. Recollect Buckman at the store was one. Claims the job's too big for one man. Says they ought to bring in half a dozen gunnies, do it up right."

Holt leaned forward. "You hear that kind of talk from any of McClendon's hired hands? Or maybe a rider from one of the ranches?"

Hornbuckle wagged his head. "Nope, can't say as I have. Mostly the townsfolk. . . . Don't think I saw that there bullet hole in your hat when you was here before. Somebody been taking pot shots at you?"

The old marshal was sharper than he let on, Jim thought. "Last night—out on the range. I was lucky. So were they."

"They?"

"Two men. Never got a close look at them."

"What you're going to be up against," Hornbuckle said with a sigh. "And you sure can't figure on your luck holding forever."

"Neither will theirs. I never got around to asking before, but have you got any hunches about who's doing the rustling in the Basin?"

"Me? Hell, I'm just a badge walking around—"

"Know that, but people talk. Thought maybe you might have heard something, or seen something—"

"Like what?"

"Well, somebody making a trip to the railhead when there was no cattle drive; or maybe a puncher flashing more money around than he ordinarily has. Things like that."

The lawman sucked on his lower lip. Then, "No, can't say as I have. Always pretty quiet around here."

"Maybe not for long," Holt said. "And when things break loose I'll be needing your help."

Hornbuckle frowned. "Me?"

"You're the law. I get to the bottom of this trouble I'll be calling on you to make the arrests, take over the prisoners and such."

A slow flush of pleasure spread over the marshal's features as if he were flattered to think he would be included in the matter.

"Why, sure. Be glad to do all I can."

Holt got to his feet. "Meantime, be obliged if you'll keep your eyes and ears open, let me know if you run into anything that's not usual. I'm doing my sleeping at McClendon's."

"I'll get word to you right quick," the lawman said, rising and following Jim to the doorway.

On the landing Holt paused, turned. "Those three hired hands of McClendon's—Reno, Munger and Billy Jay—they spend much time here in town?"

"Come in a couple, maybe three times a week, I reckon."

"At night?"

Hornbuckle shook his head. "Not lately. Heard said they was working the night shift. Do come in, how-somever, when they're on days."

"Cully Ryan usually with them?"

"Not every time. Do seem to be with them though when he comes in for something. Say, you ain't thinking maybe they got a hand in—"

"Just questions," Holt said, his eyes on the figure of Reece Oatman coming from his office. "Always try to keep up on the comings and goings of people. So long," he added and moved out into the street.

Oatman saw him, halted at the edge of the board sidewalk, a smile on his lips. He was a slim, sharp-faced man with gray hair and dark eyes. He wore a full, curved mustache along with a neatly trimmed, pointed beard.

"Jim Holt!" he said, extending his hand and pressing forward. "Heard McClendon had sent for you."

Holt accepted the greeting, faintly surprised at its warmth. He didn't remember being all that well acquainted with the one-time rancher, but supposed that now, being a man of business, Reece had acquired the necessary friendly approach.

"You making any headway?" Oatman asked.

"Not so far," Jim said, shrugging. "You get around pretty much, got any ideas?"

Oatman glanced up and down the street. Few persons were abroad, and none within hearing distance, but he lowered his voice nevertheless.

"Was I you, I'd keep my eye on that bunch that's got my old place."

"Dave Bogard and his partners?"

"Right. Things ain't been the same since they moved in."

"Sounds funny, coming from you."

"Maybe so, but they were strangers to me when I sold it to them—to Bogard himself, really. Maybe if I'd known what they were, I'd athought twice about it."

57

"There anything particular that makes you think they could be the ones doing the rustling?"

"Well . . . no. Nothing you could nail down tight. But what else could you expect from a bunch of ex-convicts?"

"Not much to that kind of argument. Such a thing as a man turning over a new leaf, going straight."

"Oh, sure! And I'm hoping that's just what they're doing. I'd sure hate to have to take that place back if something happened to them. Do get a mite nervous about it, though. Odds against them being honest are awful big. You'll have to admit that."

Holt shrugged. "Odds against folks around here giving them a chance are what's big," he said drily, and turned away. "Appreciate your getting word to me if you run across anything that might help."

"You got my promise," Oatman said breezily. "Fact is, I'm due at the McClendons' in a couple of days for dinner. I'll try to have something for you when I come out."

Holt nodded, walked on down the street to the Palace. Entering, he found the place deserted except for the bartender and a swamper cleaning up after the previous night's activities. Jim treated himself to a drink, and returning to the sorrel, took the south road out of town. He had to admit he'd accomplished little of note other than to set a few things in motion. But stirring around in the ashes of a fire quite often starts a few flames to flickering again. Oatman, who undoubtedly did do considerable moving about the Territory, was a good bet. Alerted now, the ex-rancher very easily might notice something he otherwise would pay no mind to.

The same applied to Town Marshal Pete Hornbuckle. It had pleased the old lawman to be brought into the matter, and now, without doubt, he'd start paying special attention to everyone and everything in the hopes of coming up with something of note.

Jim hoped he would. He had developed a soft spot for the old man and felt sorry for him because of the degrading position the people of the town and Basin had placed him in. When and if he laid the rustlers by the heels, he'd see to it that Pete Hornbuckle played a prominent part in the finale. Perhaps then folks would look upon their marshal in a different light.

Reaching the end of the street, Holt cut away from the beaten road, struck across open country for an embankment of bluffs lying well south of the Jicarilla Basin proper. He already had his look at the area in which the ranches sprawled and at, to a limited degree, the rough land west of them.

But the country to the south—south even of Dave Bogard's—was ground he had yet to travel and consider. Since he was in a good position to accomplish that, he had decided to take that route on his return trip to McClendon's.

Late in the morning he reached the bluffs, worked his way through the brushy, arroyo-slashed slopes at their base and climbed to the mesa above. There, for a time, he was on a broad, wind-swept plateau, and then as he rode gradually north, the land again began to break up into small canyons and washes.

There was little grass, and it was easy to see why no one had claimed the flat for range. It would seem that some master hand forming the country had placed all of the good things—grass, water, trees of consequence—in one area, the Jicarilla Basin, and had left nothing for the surrounding area.

Jim wondered if that were true of the country farther west beyond the ridge of mountains. He'd heard it was only desert, unfit for man or cattle, but he could not recall ever speaking with anyone who'd actually been there. . . . Tomorrow he'd ride that way; head west off the Basin's free range, see if it was possible to move cattle through the breaks—and find out for himself what lay beyond the ridges. He just might find something of interest.

The faint, seemingly distant bawling of cattle came to him. Frowning, he drew the sorrel to a halt, threw his glance around in a quick circle. He was somewhere south of Bogard's, he knew, since he had not as yet reached the house with its smaller buildings. But he was on Bogard range; the southeast corner marker that Dave had pointed out to him that previous night when they had gone for a short ride was behind him.

There should be no cattle in that section of the ranch. The small herd Dave and his partners were running was pastured to the west; he'd had a look at it, too. Raising himself in the stirrups, he made a second search of the surrounding country.

A shift in the faint breeze brought the bawling to him again. Calves, it sounded like. Too high pitched for grown steers. It seemed to have come from his right, from one of the numerous, small canyons that butted against a fairly high butte. Settling himself, he put the sorrel into motion, crossed a narrow saddle of flinty ground, and pulled up at its edge.

There were cattle in one of the canyons, there was no doubt of that. The sounds were clear. He gave the face of the butte a critical glance, tried to figure which of the slashes was the most likely possibility. The largest, near center, appeared to be the best bet. Spurring the sorrel, he approached the break at an angle, drew to a halt at its mouth.

It looked to be more of a wide arroyo, well filled with brush. Drawing his pistol, Jim eased the gelding forward, eyes probing the center of the sandy wash. Reaching an almost solid wall of brush, he again halted. Dismounting, he brushed the sweat from his eyes and began to work his way through the clumps of greasewood, rabbitbush, and other rank growth deeper into the arroyo. Abruptly he came to a halt against a rope-strung fence closing off the wash.

A natural corral, further made secure by a man, or men. In it were two dozen or more calves—McClendon's missing stock, he guessed. And they were on Dave Bogard's range. . . .

❄ IX ❄

A GUST OF ANGER swept through Jim Holt. He'd been lied to after all. He'd been wrong about Dave Bogard and his partners.

Moving in closer, he looked around. The calves, all

unbranded, were lean and appeared starved. A few forksful of hay had been tossed into the arroyo, but it was all pretty well trampled. There was no indication of water. There could be a spring at the head of the wash, or there possibly were some barrels, hauled in by the rustlers, placed back in the brush.

Judging from the droppings, Holt guessed the stock had been penned in the arroyo for ten days or so, perhaps even two weeks. That jibed pretty well with what McClendon had said about noting the loss of his calves.

Wheeling, his anger further irritated by the noisy bawling of the animals, he returned to the sorrel and set out for Bogard's place at a hard lope. Grim, he came into the yard, pulled up short as Dave, accompanied by Delgado, stepped through the doorway into the sunlight.

Bogard's grin faded as he had his look at Holt's face, but he said, "Step down, have a cup of coffee. Didn't expect you back so soon."

Holt made no move to dismount. "Don't think you figured me riding across your south range, either," he said coldly.

Bogard's eyes narrowed slightly. The *vaquero* moved a step to one side, getting himself from behind his partner.

"Now, what the hell's that mean?" Bogard asked.

"Where's Ivan?" Jim asked, ignoring the question.

"Looking after the herd. Where else? What about my south range?"

"Those calves you've got penned in that box

canyon—where'd you get them?"

Amazement crossed Bogard's face. He glanced to Delgado, came back to Holt. "What calves? What box canyon? What're you talking about?"

"Twenty maybe thirty head of them on your south range. All corralled up neat with a rope gate. And being fed. You trying to tell me you don't know anything about them?"

"I ain't trying," Bogard said, his voice low and distinct, "I am telling you. I don't know a damned thing about it."

Holt's eyes went to the *vaquero*. "You?"

Delgado shook his head. "I know nothing of calves."

"Neither will Ivan," Bogard said. "Whose are they?"

"Belong to McClendon. Were rustled a couple of weeks ago."

"And because you found them on my land, you figure we're the ones who rustled them."

"You think of any other explanation?"

Dave Bogard swore helplessly. Delgado shrugged, looked off across the yard. Ivan Wright, astride a bony, gray mare, was coming out of the swale west of the house. Holt waited in silence for the older man to arrive and dismount.

"Howdy," Wright said, and then gave his partners a searching glance. At once his manner changed. "You're visiting again powerful quick, seems."

"Got a good reason," Holt snapped. "You know anything about the calves penned up on your south range?"

Wright stared, threw another look at his partners, and

smiled humorlessly. "Am I supposed to?"

Bogard spat. "He thinks we stole them from McClendon. Hid them in a box canyon down there somewheres."

Ivan Wright grinned again. "Seems natural. We been blamed for about everything this side of thunder and lightning around here. Why not that?"

"You never got around to answering the question," Holt pressed quietly.

"No, goddammit—I don't know nothing about it! That what you want me to say?"

"What I want is the truth," Jim replied. "Seems strange to me that stock could be there and none of you would know anything about it."

"Not strange at all," Bogard said. "We ain't never used that part of the range. Best grazing's west of here, and we ain't got a big enough herd to do any drifting."

"Bit hard to swallow. Canyon's not five miles from here, but you never heard anything or saw anybody coming or going."

"Happens we sleep nights," Wright said. "And I misdoubt whoever put them critters there done it in the daytime."

"If it was somebody else doing it," Holt said, "they'd have picked a better place—one where the calves wouldn't be found."

"Maybe that's the point," Bogard said, rubbing at his jaw. "Maybe that's just what somebody wanted."

Delgado began to nod his head. "It is so. Who finds these calves will blame us—like you are doing, *señor.* It is the way it was planned."

"I'm betting you're right, Del," Wright said. "Only you won't get this law and order gent to believe that. He's believing what he sees. Calves were stole, he finds them on our range. Adds up to one thing—we done the rustling."

Bogard's gaze was locked on Holt. "That what you think, Jim?"

"Pretty hard to see it any other way. And it sure as hell is what everybody else in the Basin is going to think."

Dave Bogard shrugged, looked away. Wright swore, crossed his arms and faced Holt belligerently.

"Well, then, what's next? You aiming to haul us all in for—"

"What I want you to do," Jim cut in sharply, "is ride down there, turn those calves out and drive them back onto McClendon's range. And I want it done now!"

Bogard came back around quickly. "And that's the end of it?"

"I'm giving you the benefit of the doubt. Could be somebody planted them there trying to throw the blame on you. I don't know, and—"

"But you're still telling McClendon about it—"

"No choice. A bunch of calves like that just don't drop out of the sky."

"So the next thing we can be looking for is a lynching party riding up the slope," Wright said in a sarcastic voice. "Hell bent on ridding the country of us rustlers."

"Be nothing like that. McClendon turned this whole deal over to me. I call the shots. When I tell him I don't want you bothered, he'll listen."

"You going to let him think we done the stealing?"

"I'll tell him exactly what I found and how you explained it—and that I figured you had the benefit of the doubt coming. That'll satisfy him."

"Maybe," Ivan Wright muttered. "But I reckon it's neither here nor there. The whole thing was bound to come a cropper sooner or later. Was just too good to last, us living the way a man ought to live."

"It's not finished for you," Holt said. "But main thing is to get those calves back onto Circle X range before somebody else runs across them. Could be what the plan is."

Bogard nodded, moved toward his horse. Delgado and Wright turned to follow. The older man paused.

"Was thinking, we bump into some of McClendon's bunch, they ain't going to wait for no explaining."

"I'll be riding with you," Holt said. "Leave the talking to me."

Wright's thin shoulders stirred. "All right, mister. We'll do it like you say. Only it ain't the talking I'm worrying about, it's the shooting that's apt to come."

"Be no gunplay," Jim assured him. "I'll see to that."

By the time they had choused all the calves from the brush, there were forty-one in the bunch. Most were in fair condition except for one that somehow injured a leg and had difficulty in keeping up with the others when the drive got underway. That particular dogie ended up a crosswise passenger sharing the saddle with Nestor Delgado.

Jim Holt rode out in front of the herd where he could

66

be readily seen by anyone encountered on the range, while Bogard and the others kept the calves tightly bunched and moving steadily.

They crossed into Circle X range and reached a small sink well down in a narrow valley where the calves, evidently suffering for water, broke loose and stampeded wildly to reach the marshy ground with its shallow pools.

Dave Bogard, Delgado, and Ivan Wright split off there. Making no comment, simply wheeling about after the *vaquero* had unloaded the crippled calf, they rode back toward the south.

Jim watched them go in brooding silence. That he had lost their friendship was apparent, and he supposed he could not blame them for how they felt. But he had done the only thing possible under the circumstances; one thing they were overlooking in their indignation was that he again had gone out on a limb for them. Had any of the Basin ranchers or their crew discovered the corralled calves, the matter would have been handled differently.

❊ X ❊

"Y OU—WHAT?" Wade McClendon said in a strangled voice.

"Just what I told you," Holt replied, anger rising. The events of the past few hours left him in no mood for having his judgment questioned by McClendon or anyone else.

"You telling me you found stock of mine on them

outlaws' range and you don't aim to bring them in for rustling?"

Cully Ryan and half a dozen other riders including Joe Reno, lounging near the bunkhouse, were listening intently. They began to move in closer to where Holt and the rancher were standing.

"No proof they had anything to do with penning up those calves," Jim said. "Claimed they didn't. I figure they're telling the truth."

"Well, I don't!" McClendon snapped. "Neither will any other rancher in the Basin."

"If that's how you feel, then you've got your job back," Holt said, hanging tight to his temper.

"Don't see as we need him any longer anyway, Mr. McClendon," Ryan said, breaking into the conversation. "Seems we got our answer."

"Them convicts," Joe Reno muttered, wagging his head. "Just like we always figured. Best thing we can do is grab us up some ropes and give them what they got coming."

Holt swung his hard glance to the puncher. "You got a reason for shutting them up quick?"

"Don't need no reason for stringing up a cattle rustler."

Ryan said, "Ease off, Joe," and then turned back to McClendon. "Way I see it, there ain't no doubt now they're the ones who've been doing the rustling—else they wouldn't have had all them calves hid away, holding them until they were big enough to mix in with the rest of their herd. If we don't take steps to stop them, they'll be right back at it again."

"You'll be lynching the wrong men," Jim said tautly. "You'd be doing it because they used to be outlaws, not because they're rustlers."

"The only man looking at it that way is you," Ryan commented. "And I reckon that's because they're old friends of yours. Said so yourself."

"Not exactly. Never met Wright or Delgado before. But it makes no difference. You can't go flying off the handle, pull a stunt like that with no more proof than we've got."

One of the older riders in the group shrugged, spat. "All depends on what you think is proof," he said. "Now, them calves hid off on their range, I'd say that was plenty of proof."

"Not according to the law—"

"We're the law here in Jicarilla Basin," Wade McClendon declared, coming back into the discussion. "Always have been, expect we always will be."

"Doubt that," Holt said, "but we're talking about right now. I'll lay it out plain. I don't want anybody bothering Dave Bogard—"

"You don't want!" Cully Ryan echoed. "Just who the hell you think you are, anyway?"

"I'm the man hired to stop the rustling in this country," Holt answered coolly. "Was told I could do it my way—and there'd be no second-guessing, especially from the hired help."

"Well, I expect you're about to get unhired," Ryan said drily. "We know all we need—"

"Never mind, Cully," McClendon broke in. "Just simmer down. I'm still running this ranch, and it'll be me who says what's what."

The Circle X foreman frowned. "But there ain't no use fiddling around about it. We figured all the time it was them. Now we got proof—"

"Seems to me you're plenty anxious to pin all the trouble the Basin's had on Bogard," Jim said, eyeing the puncher narrowly.

Ryan's color darkened. "You accusing me of being a rustler?"

Holt's gaze met Cully's, held. "I've done some wondering about it. . . . You along with some others."

Ryan lunged, fists swinging. Jim swept the man's arms aside, shoved hard, sent him sprawling into the dust. Ryan was up instantly and coming back. McClendon caught him by the shoulder.

"Cool off, Cully. Fighting amongst ourselves ain't going to get us nowheres."

"Nobody calls me a rustler," Ryan gritted through clenched teeth. "I'll—"

"He didn't say that. Just said he'd wondered about it, same as he has about a few others."

"Same thing—"

McClendon sighed heavily, glanced at Holt. "Was maybe a mite strong. You care to beg his pardon, do some explaining?"

Jim Holt shook his head. "Don't figure either one's necessary. And I'll do any needful apologizing when this thing's cleaned up. Not about to before."

The rancher raised his arm, sleeved the sweat from his face, and stared off toward the hills. "You that sure it ain't Bogard, Jim?"

"Sure enough that I did what I did knowing how you'd feel about it—and sure enough to keep on looking. If it turns out I'm wrong, I'll haul them in to the marshal same as I would some stranger."

McClendon said, absently, "Yeh, I reckon you would at that. . . . How much more time you going to need?"

"Little hard to figure that."

"Better not be long. Once word about them calves gets bandied through the Basin, hell's going to start popping."

"If I get some kind of a break—"

"You done got it," Joe Reno said, "One that's plain as the nose on your face. Only you're covering up, not wanting to see it or do anything about it because it's your friends that's got their foot in it. You're even trying to push the blame off on Cully—and me and some others."

"Glad you mentioned yourself," Holt said and suddenly whipped off his hat. Pointing to the blackened, torn place left by the bushwhacker's bullet, he added, "Know what that is?"

The rider shrugged. "Bullet hole, I reckon."

"What it is, all right. Somebody took three shots at me last night down near the bluffs. Mind telling me where you were about midnight?"

Reno swallowed, looked around at the men ranged about him. "Now he's accusing me of trying to bushwhack him! Mr. McClendon, I think you got yourself a crazy man on this job!"

"Where were you?" Holt pressed.

"Was working, that's where. Night riding the herd.

Me, and Austin, and Earl Munger, and Curly Yates—couple of others."

"There anybody can prove you never rode off at any time—left the cattle?"

It was a question that meant nothing, Jim knew. All the riders were absent from each other at times since it was in the nature of their duties to move around, maintain a watch over the stock.

"Why, sure. It'll be real easy," Reno replied. "Ask Munger or Billy Jay, most any of the boys nighthawking."

Holt's lips parted in a faint smile. He hadn't expected Joe Reno to have a ready alibi since none was really needed; the job itself served as such. . . . He had a sudden feeling that he had struck pay dirt, that an earlier hunch was gaining in strength.

Reaching into his pocket he produced the spent rifle cartridges, displayed them in the palm of his hand. "Bushwhacker forgot these in his hurry last night. Found them plenty interesting."

Both Cully Ryan and Reno took a step nearer for a better look, but Jim closed his hand, thrust the casings back into his pocket.

"Not ready yet to talk about them," he said.

McClendon had been standing by, studying him in silence. "You never told me nothing about an ambush when we were talking this morning," he said accusingly.

"Didn't figure there was any need."

"Maybe you forgot to mention it because it could've been your friends. Could've decided they'd best shut you up before you told anybody about them calves."

Holt smiled to himself. He had expected Wade McClendon to voice that exact conclusion. Shaking his head, he said, "No, wasn't them. This happened before that. Were two men. One suckered me in to where his partner was holed up in the bluffs."

"Well, one thing for sure," the rancher said, "you can figure it was the rustlers."

"No doubt, and it means I'm tromping on somebody's corns. Now, where do we stand? You going to take it for granted that Bogard's the one stealing cattle, or do you want me to stay on the job until I find out who it really is?"

McClendon spread his hands in a gesture of resignation. "We want the one's who're doing it, sure. You claim it ain't that bunch on the Oatman place, and I got to admit there's only a happenstance case against them. Only sensible thing I can see is for you to keep on working at it."

Jim Holt nodded. "All I want to know. Just keep your shirt on. Something tells me I'm about to plow up some snakes."

I T WAS HOT in the bunkhouse. Sprawled on his bed, dressed only in pants and undershirt, Jim Holt brushed at the sweat on his forehead and thought about the day. Elsewhere in the stuffy quarters men slept, snored; but the place was almost deserted. Several of the punchers had elected to ride into Butte for a bit of recreation; others were simply off somewhere waiting for the night's coolness to come.

They were all avoiding him as they would blackleg. His veiled accusations and hints that any of them could be involved in the rustling had made him considerably less than popular—but he was worrying very little about that. Doing the kind of jobs he ordinarily was hired to do, left no room for friendships. It was a lonely way of life at best.

He was far from sleep. The belief that he was close to something important dogged his mind persistently and refused to let him rest. He needed only to put two and two together and come up with some answers, but somehow he couldn't find the starting point.

Hunches, intuition, sure; but they didn't count except as signs along a devious trail that would lead him to an eventual solution. Why couldn't he sort out all the things that were scurrying about in his head, put his finger on the necessary facts? What was standing in the way, blinding him to what he should see easily?

Restless, he sat up. The puncher two bunks down the line was snoring so hard the noise seemed to rattle the boards in the walls. Stepping into his boots, he dug into his shirt pocket for his sack of tobacco and wheat papers and rose, making for the door. Maybe a smoke would settle him down, induce sleep. He needed it. Tomorrow was going to be a hard day.

Moving out onto the landing, he stopped, sucked deep at the fresh air. Then selecting a slip of the thin paper, he tapped a quantity of powdery tobacco into its curved trough, rolled it into a thin cylinder between his thumb and forefinger.

Moistening and tapering the cigarette, he fired a

match with his nail, puffed the tobacco into life. Stepping down from the landing, he sauntered lazily toward a broadly spreading cottonwood tree under which someone had thoughtfully built a bench.

He drew abreast of the corner of the bunkhouse, halted as the scuff of boots caught his attention. Before he could turn he felt the hard, round muzzle of a pistol jab into his spine. Another clubbed him sharply on the side of the head, set his brain to reeling. Faintly, he heard a voice in the darkness.

"Take him around back. Time we're done with him he'll be ready to quit—ride on."

Was it Cully Ryan's voice? It was difficult to concentrate—he couldn't be sure.

❈ XI ❈

THERE WERE THREE—no, four of them. Holt stumbled again as one of the men struck him on the head a second time with a pistol. His legs wobbled, but he shook off the giddiness, stayed upright.

"Here'll be fine," a voice said as they halted in a pool of blackness behind the bunkhouse.

Immediately a fist drove into Holt's belly, exploding breath from his lungs. The pain seemed to clear his head as he buckled forward, and suddenly a towering anger was boiling through him.

With a powerful heave, he wrenched free of the hands that gripped his arms and lashed out with a balled fist. He felt the shock of contact, heard a grunt, and had the satisfaction of knowing he'd connected solidly. Instantly fists began to hammer at him from all sides, and for a full minute there was only the scuff of boots, muttered curses, the dry slapping sound of flesh meeting flesh as he traded blows blindly with his unseen assailants.

Holding my own, he thought grimly, and began to work his way backwards toward the yard where light from one of the windows would give him a look at the men swarming around him. A fist jabbed against his jaw, rocked his head. He swore. It was the first sharp blow he'd taken high; so far his body had been absorbing all the punishment.

He tried to pivot, swing a long right, nail one of the shifting shadows. He missed, went off balance. Fists pounded at his back, his neck, his shoulders. A knee, corning up from somewhere, caught him in the ribs and he was suddenly on the ground. A pointed toe dug into his side, the force of it bringing a gasp of pain to his lips. Again unbridled rage swept him. He fought his way to his feet, grabbed for a fleeting shape directly before him.

His fingers caught at cloth. He struck out with his free hand. The figure wilted, began to sink and he shoved it away. A blow slammed into his neck. He spun, felt something graze his head. The one using a pistol as a club was at it again.

He jerked back, collided solidly with someone behind him. Holt's heavier bulk knocked the man aside, sent him cursing to the hardpack. He continued to backpedal, trying again to reach the light. He had no idea who his attackers were, could only guess. . . . They were playing it smart, giving him no clue to their identities by using their voices.

A sudden rush carried Holt off his feet. Two or three of them had come at him together. He went down hard, flat in the dust. Instantly they were all upon him, pounding at his body, slapping, kicking. Protecting his head with his arms, he heaved to one side, rolled over, got to his knees. A blow to the jaw dazed him. He swore, shook off the mist, struggled once more to his feet.

From somewhere out of the night a voice called: "What's going on out there?"

There was a pause as if his assailants had pulled back, apparently alarmed by the protesting inquiry. It could be McClendon, he realized. Shaking his head again, Holt lunged forward, grabbing for one of the shadows. In almost that same instant, a pistol butt crashed into the back of his skull and he pitched down into deeper darkness.

He was out only moments, he guessed. Lifting his head he glanced around, listened. The men had gone and there was only silence of the night. Painfully, stiffly, he got to his feet, still slightly dazed, but fully aware of the dull aches that throbbed throughout his body.

Walking slowly, he moved out of the blackness behind the bunkhouse, made his way to the horse trough a dozen yards away. Dropping to his knees, he lowered his head into the cold water. Full consciousness returned in a rush.

Rising, he stripped off what little clothing he was wearing, and stark naked, climbed into the wooden trough. The shock of it blasted breath from him in a loud gasp, but he stayed put, almost totally immersed, feeling a gradual decreasing of the pain and soreness that was locking into his body.

Finally he rose dripping from the water, and shaking the dust from his undershirt, scrubbed himself dry. Pulling on his pants and boots, he returned to the bunkhouse feeling considerably better physically, but smoldering inwardly with anger.

Halting inside the doorway, he scanned the room. The men who had been there earlier were still in their bunks, apparently had slept through the disturbance unmoved. But Jim Holt wanted to be sure.

Moving down the aisle he looked closely at each rider, searching for the telltale bruises and scratches he knew that would be on their faces if they had taken part in the incident. He found none—and that was what he had expected.

The four who jumped him had been outside. Either they had planned the attack and had been waiting for him, or else, seeing him standing alone in the yard smoking his cigarette, had acted on impulse and taken advantage of the opportunity. That sounded the more logical.

Tired, he made his way to his bunk and stretched out. No matter. . . . He'd have his look at the crew when they gathered for breakfast. He'd have no trouble picking out the men who'd crawled him; he'd gotten in quite a few good wallops himself before the one using his gun as a club had ended the fight.

But at the table that next morning he learned nothing. The majority of the crew had already ridden out to take up the day's work, and the men he found there were devoid of scars.

All looked at him intently and curiously, missing none of the swelling and dark patches on his face as he sat down. There were no comments, however. The wall of silent hostility that had sprung up the first day he had arrived at McClendon's was more in evidence now than ever.

As he filled his plate, Holt glanced to the cook waiting nearby with a pot of coffee. "Seems everybody pulled out mighty early. Some reason?"

"All I do is the grub fixing," the old man said.

Two of the riders at the table pushed back their chairs, reached for their hats and slammed out into the yard.

"Cully with them?"

The cook shrugged. "Don't rightly know 'cause I never pay no close attention. They come dragging in, then go dragging out. . . ."

"You can do better than that," Jim said, his tone hardening. "Think about it."

"Am thinking."

"What about Munger and Reno—and that young Texan, Billy Jay? Were they here earlier?"

"Don't recollect seeing them. Could've been."

The cook, too, Holt thought. If he had to take a count of friends on the Circle X, he'd need no fingers at all. After yesterday he guessed even Wade McClendon was against him, was only standing by because he had made a commitment. But he supposed, after more or less implying that anyone on the ranch could be mixed up in the rustling, he could expect it to be no different. He turned again to the older man.

"Don't reckon you noticed anybody around who looked like he got himself in a scrap last night?"

"Sure didn't," the cook replied laconically.

Holt laughed, giving rise to a stab of pain in his jaw. "You don't see much of anything, do you, Cookie? I think maybe it'd be a real good idea to take up a collection, buy you a pair of specs. . . ."

The man cocked his head to one side. "Maybe. But I still wouldn't go poking my snout into something that ain't none of my business."

"This is your business. It goes busted, you're out of a job."

"Not saying it ain't, but when somebody comes rearing in here, saying things, riling everybody up, I ain't about to give him no help."

"You've got your ropes crossed, friend," Holt said, abruptly cold. "I'm doing what I was hired to do."

"That give you leave to call everybody a rustler while all the time you're protecting the ones who really done the stealing just on account of them being friends of your'n?"

The last of the crew seated at the table rose, paused long enough to favor Holt with hard stares, and then moved on through the doorway.

"Wrong again," Jim said, "but there's no use trying to explain it. I'll—"

He hesitated as the pounding of a horse racing into the yard caught him up short. A man called, "Where's that there fellow Holt?"

Rising, Jim stepped out into the yard quickly. "Right here."

The puncher spurred his horse in close. "Name's Mitch. Damion King sent me. Damned rustlers got about fifty head of beef last night. He's wanting you to come."

"Be right with you," Holt said, and started for the corral at a run.

❦ XII ❦

BEVAN AND CARL JOHNSON were at the D Bar K when Holt rode in. With King, they were standing on the porch of the low, rambling ranch house awaiting his arrival. King came out into the yard in a rush as Jim halted at the hitchrack.

"Was prime stock they got!" he shouted. "Little jag I had fattening off to itself. Reckon there ain't no doubt now about that bunch at the Oatman place!"

Holt was conscious of the close looks all the ranchers were giving his bruised features, but they asked for no explanation and he offered none. Their minds were centered on the rustling, anyway.

"What makes you so sure it was Bogard?"

"Who else can it be?" King demanded. "Them calves of McClendon's are all the proof I need."

"No proof of anything there," Holt replied. "Slow down now and tell me a little more about what's happened. Was last night, Mitch said."

"Last night, yesterday, maybe even the night before. Ain't sure. Nobody noticed the stock was gone until this morning. Was there day before yesterday—know that for a fact. Rode out to have a look at them myself."

"Where were they grazing?"

"Due west, about five miles."

"On that open range?"

"Yeah. Been running stock there right along. McClendon's got some stuff south of me. So's Jack."

Jim glanced to Bevan. "You lose any?"

The rancher shook his head. "Ain't sure, yet. Not easy to tell right off. I'll know later."

Holt lifted the sorrel's reins. "About fifty head, all branded?" he said to King.

"Fifty, more or less. And they was branded. I got enough boys around to make up a posse if you—"

"No need for that. I'll handle it alone," Jim said. He started to pull away, noted the scowling disapproval on the rancher's face. "You understand? I'll take care of it. I don't want anybody flying off on his own, spoiling everything. This maybe's the break I've been waiting for."

"Waste of time," Johnson said. "That's all your hunting around's going to be. My guess is you'll find those steers at Bogard's."

"The waste of time would be going to Bogard's. If he was fool enough to rustle cattle after I found those calves on his range only yesterday, he sure as hell wouldn't drive King's stock right back onto his own land."

"Still figure it'd be smart to ride over there, have a look. Going to give me a lot of satisfaction nailing the hides of them convicts to the wall."

"Better be sure they're guilty first," Holt said drily. "Now, stay put—all of you. When I need help I'll ask for it."

Damion King shot a glance at Johnson and Bevan and then shrugged. "All right, but you'd better come up with something. I've lost all the goddamn cows I aim to."

"Same goes for me," Johnson said.

Holt pulled away from the rack, headed direct west. He rode at a steady lope, his mind on Bogard and the missing cattle. He was certain the man and his two partners would not be guilty of the theft; if they actually were the rustlers preying upon Jicarilla Basin stock, which he did not believe, they wouldn't have struck so soon after the incident of the calves as he'd pointed out to Johnson.

Unless. . . . Holt frowned as a thought came to him. Unless such was exactly what Dave Bogard wanted him and the ranchers to think. He shook himself. It was hard to accept that—harder yet to believe Bogard had lied to him.

A time later he topped out a high roll of land and looked down upon a fairly good herd grazing near a water hole. Immediately on his appearance two riders separated from the cattle and rode out leisurely to intercept him. As he drew near, they split, and shortly he was in between them with one facing him from the left, the other from the right. Both were astride D Bar K horses.

Jim pulled the sorrel to a stop, allowed the punchers to study him briefly, then said, "Name's Holt. I'm looking into the rustling that's been going on around here."

The men were silent for a few moments, and then the older of the pair said, "Heard of you."

"Reckon it's him," the other rider said. "Sure big enough, anyway."

Jim felt their curious gaze as they took in his appearance. The younger puncher was unable to contain himself.

"You walk yourself into a mowing machine, or something?"

Holt grinned. "Me and a few friends were playing ring around the rosy last night. Got a mite rough. . . . You tell me where that bunch of steers that got rustled were grazing?"

The older man twisted about on his saddle, pointed to twin hillocks a mile or so in the distance.

"Was the yonder side of them mounds. Little hollow there. But you won't find no sign. We done looked."

"No tracks at all?"

"Nope. Them danged rustlers pulled the same stunt again—drove some other stock along the flat between the hollow and the rocks, tromped out everything a man could follow."

Jim considered that for a time. Then, "You two been riding herd along here regularly?"

"Nope. Just since this morning. Spelled off Henry Link and Casey Kleven."

"Then you don't know exactly when those steers were run off either. Seems to be doubt whether it was last night or sooner."

"They're gone. That's all I know."

Holt said, "Much obliged," and rode on.

The fact that no one ever saw any strangers, noticed any dust, heard any sounds of stock on the move again came to mind and struck Jim as peculiar. It was only reasonable to believe that someone in the Basin had to be aware of something. A herd of steers being driven across the range was bound to draw attention—day or night.

Unless the cattle were not moved across the range, but instead were driven into that area everyone thought impossible to enter.

Jim raised his glance to the wild, rugged country west of the Basin. He had given it consideration before, had planned to have a better look at the maze of brush, rock, and canyons that led up to the towering mountains in the distance. The answer could lie there. Several of the ranchers had spoken of investigating the area, but in the same breath had admitted their search had been only halfhearted; they simply took it for granted that cattle could not be trailed through such country.

But Jim Holt never accepted anything on such a basis, and now as he rode on across the gentle swells and smooth flats of the Basin itself, he discovered a conviction growing within him. And then doubt arose. . . . A herd would leave tracks as it crossed on its way to the brakes. Or would it?

He looked more closely at the ground beneath the sorrel's hooves. It was covered with a tough, springy grass. Only here and there were barren places where passing steers would leave marks. There would be prints, he decided, but only a few and well scattered. All he need do was search them out.

He reached the twin hills, rode down to where King had quartered his special bunch of steers. It was somewhat of a sink, akin to the water hole where he had left McClendon's calves, except it was considerably larger and with a better stand of grass.

Coming in from the near side, he guided the sorrel down to the edge of the soft ground and there began to circle the area slowly. On the far rim he came to a halt. The muddy ground showed where the herd had been bunched, and then moved out—pointing toward the south, not to the west as he had expected.

Puzzled, he began to follow. Cattle traveling in that direction were certain to be seen by riders looking after other herds. Abruptly he halted. Understanding came to him. Ahead now, instead of the distinct prints of the closely bunched jag of cattle, was a welter of tracks. It was as he'd been told, the rustlers were smart; they erased all signs of their activities by driving other steers over the trail left by the stock they were stealing.

Suddenly impatient, Holt cut left, cantered due east to a low ridge and looked back across the flat. Several hundred steers were grazing below him. Spurring the sorrel, he rode in close, eyes seeking the brand on the stock. . . . Circle X. . . . McClendon's beef. Likely they were the ones that had been driven over the trail left by

King's cattle. Nudging the gelding, he moved along the edge of the herd seeking the men who should be watching the stock. He found no one. The herd was on its own.

Wheeling, he headed back for the point where the tracks of the rustled cattle had been wiped out. With conditions as they were, Jim thought it strange that no punchers were with McClendon's cattle; normally a man could expect to find a close watch being kept everywhere. But there could be more of the same herd farther to the east, and the riders might be at that point; shortly they could swing back, and continuing a system of running back and forth, keep an eye on all of the herd. . . . Perhaps that was the way it was being done.

Moving to the edge of the tracks, Jim (following his hunch) cut directly west, and crossing a narrow strip of ground that sloped up to the extreme edge of the Basin, came to the rock-studded shoulder that separated the grass land from the ragged brakes country beyond.

He found no tracks there other than those made by strays. Thoughtfully he studied the area. To continue west across the flinty shoulder of almost solid granite would get a man nowhere since it butted up against an almost vertical slope. More palisades blocked the way to the north.

If the rustled cattle were being driven into the brakes, there would have to be some sort of an entrance farther south. Putting the gelding into motion, Holt rode on, keeping to the edge of the Basin, eyes raking the wall of rock and brush along the far side of the shoulder.

A quarter mile later he pulled up. A break in the tangled undergrowth, like a narrow aisle, had caught his attention. Dropping from the saddle, he walked out onto the shoulder, began to examine the ground carefully. After a moment he straightened up, satisfaction flowing through him. In a small, palm-size patch of soil between the rocks, he had found the imprint of a steer's hoof.

He had part of the answer. Stolen cattle, at first deliberately pointed south on the range to mislead anyone attempting to follow, were veered right after a short distance and driven onto the shoulder. Other stock was then herded across their trail to wipe out all evidence of the cattle's movements, particularly the spot where the steers left the Basin proper.

The rustled stock was then moved along the shoulder. Such would be a slow, hazardous task for cattle since the surface of the ground over which they walked would be slippery under their hooves. Here again the rustlers had displayed their cunning; the journey was short, calculated to be just long enough from the point of entry to the aisle in the brush to leave no telltale sign. . . . That was the way of it, assuming the opening in the brush meant something.

Urging the gelding on, Holt rode onto the shoulder, entered the narrow break. Brush and rock crowded in from both sides for several hundred feet, and then the trail dipped down and began to follow out an almost flat hogback that angled off to the right.

Keeping his eyes on the hard, barren soil, he moved on slowly. Driving cattle through such country would be a difficult task and losses would be considerable; but there are no costs where a rustler is concerned, and he could afford to lose a few head to the steep canyons dropping away on either side of the rocky trail.

The ridge wound on, began then to slant more toward the end of the mountains. The brush became more tangled, the boulders larger, and then abruptly the hogback ended. Holt stopped, surprise running through him. Cutting in from his right was a narrow side canyon. A small stream flowed along its floor.

He pulled off his hat, mopped at the sweat beading his forehead. He hadn't known about the creek, of course, doubted if anyone in the Basin was aware of its presence. He was a good ten miles from the range, he guessed, and likely no one had ever ventured that far into what was considered worthless land.

The canyon walls offered no trail and he was forced to ride down into the stream itself. It wasn't deep, barely covered the sorrel's hooves, and in no place was over ten feet in width. But it would offer easy passage for cattle making it that far, and encouraged by that thought, Jim Holt rode on.

The canyon curved to the west as it cut deeper into the hills. High palisades began to shape up on either side, slashed by crevices from which scraggy shrubs and rock daisies clung precariously. The quick flash of tan and white across a hump of rock warned Holt of a mountain lion's presence; and once, a coyote darted across in front of him, hurdling the creek with ease.

It was shadowy and cool in the depths of the canyon, almost like evening, and he glanced through the banks of foliage to the sun. It was no later than three o'clock, he supposed.

Regardless of time, he wasn't turning back. He'd come too far now and, if necessary, he'd spend the night in the mountains, resume the search when daylight again made it possible.

The sorrel was beginning to tire after the continued use he'd been put to. Noting a small finger of land jutting into the stream, Jim pulled out, halted. Dismounting, he left the gelding to browse and climbed a short ways up the steep slope to where he could get a reaching look at the country ahead.

The canyon appeared to wind on, bearing always to the west. There was no diminishing in the rugged character of the country, and it was possible he was entering an even wilder section. He located a thin ribbon of silver well in the distance; the stream evidently maintained its course.

He rested the gelding for a half hour and then resumed the trail of water. Some time later he became aware that the steady falling away of the canyon began to check and the floor was becoming more or less level. Rounding a sharp bend Holt saw they were heading onto a broad saddle that swung between two opposing buttes to form a massive, gate-like entrance to the country beyond. Likely a valley, he thought, as the high lifting bulk of another mountain lay to the far side.

A full hour after he'd had his first glimpse of the change, he reached the saddle. With the sun now sliding swiftly toward the horizon, he worked his way across to the edge.

A glow of satisfaction filled him as he drew to a stop. Below, in a small basin, was a cabin.

❊ XIII ❊

I T WAS A BARREN, deserted-appearing place; a solitary, weather-lashed house around which weeds grew in wild abandon. Two or three small outbuildings, a corral with a chute-like attachment off one side—and nothing more. But someone lived there; a thin streamer of smoke was twisting upwards from the chimney.

Once it had been occupied by a homesteader, Jim guessed, but the uncertainty of the elements combined with the utter isolation of the area had likely united to wash away the dream of some hopeful soul, and thus it had been forsaken. Now, it would seem at first blush, that it had become an ideal headquarters for rustlers.

Holt could see cattle in the corral, probably fifty head or so, and chances were good they were the ones so recently stolen from Damion King. Ranchers in the Basin would be surprised to learn of the place, less than twenty miles from their range. No doubt it was the forbidding brakes and mountains that blocked their thoughts, caused them to assume the area was completely desolate and uninhabited.

The rustlers had worked a very clever scheme. By moving the cattle off the range onto the rock-paved surface of the shoulder and then down into a stream, they left no trail at all. Thus the herds, always small, seemed to completely vanish without a trace. Brought to this point, brands would be altered and then the stock would be driven south to a railhead other than the one used by the Basin ranchers.

But who were the rustlers? Who was the man at the head of the gang? It had to be someone well acquainted with the Jicarilla Basin—someone who knew which herd was the most accessible and when the time would be the most opportune for a swift, silent raid.

Dave Bogard? Undoubtedly he and his partners could make such information known to themselves. It would be easy to drift about the range during the night, avoid the riders on nighthawk duty, and size up the herds. Simpler yet for them to take the stock down the trail to this remote pocket, change brands, and drive them to a shipping point or to some distant rancher who wasn't particular about whom he bought cattle from.

And since no one ever visited Bogard's, actually avoided the three men because of what they had been in the past, they were in a position to come and go as they pleased—be absent for days on end, in fact—with no one being the wiser. It fit only too well.

But that didn't jibe with what had taken place behind the bunkhouse that previous night. It hadn't been Dave Bogard and Wright and Nestor Delgado who had jumped him; it had been men from McClendon's crew aided, perhaps, by others from different ranches.

They'd worked him over because he was treading on someone's toes, getting too close to the identity of those doing the rustling. At least, he figured that was the reason. . . . Could it be, instead, that they had taken it in mind to simply punish him for the hard words he'd spoken, the half accusations he'd tossed out in the hope of starting someone to worrying and making a misstep? Personal integrity was a touchy factor with most punchers and to have it challenged was no small insult. Such could have been the reason he was jumped. And if so, the finger of suspicion pointed more and more at Dave Bogard.

Why sweat over it? The answer lay at the cabin in the basin and would be his as soon as darkness fell. It would be no chore to slip down the slope, work his way through the tall weeds to the house, and have a look at whoever was inside. Then he could stop specu- lating, guessing. . . . Best he have a look at the trail off the saddle before dark, however. It could be a tricky one.

It was far from that. Moving to the lip of the swale, he saw where the cattle had pulled out of the creek which angled to the right and began a hurried, tum- bling descent over a series of ledges to the valley below.

The path itself cut to the opposite direction, followed a gradual decline as it wound back and forth on a fairly smooth slope. Cattle would have no difficulty moving along it, Jim saw, as he rode the sorrel along its gentle grade.

He halted again, this time in the fringe of brush and scrub oak at the edge of the clearing in which the house and other structures stood. It was still an hour until complete dark, and there was nothing to do but wait.

Accordingly, he pulled well back from the trail in the event any rider passed that way, and settled down.

He could hear the cattle bawling restlessly. Shortly a door slammed. Rising, Holt peered through the weeds at the house. An elderly man had come into the yard and was moving toward a pile of hay near the corral. Taking up a fork, he tossed several bunches into the enclosure. Then turning to a crude flume that was carrying water in from the creek, he released the block of wood that served as a floodgate and permitted a stream to pour into a trough built along the inside of the pen.

He lounged against the corral for a time until the trough had filled, and then replacing the wood block, headed back for the house. Holt strained for a better look at the man. . . . A stranger. No one he had ever seen before. The door slammed again and Holt settled back once more.

At last it was dark. Taking up the sorrel's reins, Jim led him out of the brush, and keeping to the blind side of the house where only shuttered windows broke the wall, moved in close. Stopping behind a clump of cedars, he tied the gelding securely, and then crouching low, made his way through the rabbitbush and sage to where he was opposite the cattle-filled corral.

He could see the back of the house from that point, could easily keep an eye on the door. A lamp had been lit and the man he'd seen earlier was moving about, preparing a meal, in what was evidently the kitchen.

Crossing a small strip of open ground, Holt drew in close to the side of the corral. Leaning through the space between poles, he examined the nearest steer.

The brand on the animal's hip was a D Bar K. . . . Damion King's rustled stock! He had felt sure of it from the crest of the slope. There was no question now.

The chute-like arrangement on the side of the pen was a few steps farther on. Curious, he moved to it, found it to be a narrow, slatted affair with sliding cross-bars at each end. His eyes then saw the blackened area and charred remains of several fires.

Nearby stood a bucket from which protruded the handles of branding irons. He squatted, examined the tools. There were circles, crosses, straight lines of varying lengths, a trailing s—running irons used to alter brands. The rustlers had a complete selection; no doubt could change effectively the mark of any rancher and do a first class job of it.

That was what the chute was for. He realized that in the next moment. A steer would be hazed out of the corral into the narrow enclosure. The sliding bars would be shot into place before and behind it, locking the animal in. A man with the iron most suitable to changing the brand would then go to work, doing his chore efficiently and quickly since the steer would be pinned unmoving in the chute. The job finished, the front bar would be pulled, the animal released and another steer hustled into position.

A smart man had worked out that arrangement, and it was a system that would enable two or three men to brand a small herd in a very short time. Holt grinned wryly into the darkness. Whoever it was that headed up the rustlers was no ordinary, run-of-the-mill cowhand. Likely he'd be hard to track down.

Pivoting, Jim retraced his steps along the corral, cut back through the weeds and made his way to the corner of the house. His view of the kitchen door was closed off from this position, and dissatisfied with that, he hunched low and crossed over to a deeply shadowed patch of ground behind a shed at the edge of the yard.

Now he could see the man inside the house again. He was sitting at a table, a cup of coffee before him. Once he turned, looked toward the door as if expecting someone. Holt's view was unimpaired from where he crouched and he had a straight-on look at the man's face. An absolute stranger. . . .

Could he be the head of the rustling gang? There certainly would be others—men who drove the cattle off the range, down through the canyon to the corral; men, possibly the same, who handled the branding irons and then later trailed the stock to market.

Since only small jags of cattle were usually involved in the rustling, it would appear that a limited number of men were engaged in the operation—half a dozen at most. If the same group handled all of the chores, half that number would be sufficient. . . . Bogard, Wright and Delgado, plus the man in the kitchen . . . four . . . the thought popped into Jim Holt's mind subconsciously. It seemed that everything led—

Abruptly he came to attention. The dull thud of an oncoming horse approaching from the south caught his attention. Suddenly tense, he crouched lower in the shadows. Maybe this would be someone he'd recognize.

❊ XIV ❊

HOLT SWORE SOFTLY. Another stranger. He watched the rider pull up to the hitchrack, dismount in the rectangle of yellow light coming through the kitchen doorway.

The man inside moved to the opening, peered into the night. "That you, Cass?"

"Yeh, Jared, it's me," the rider answered in a weary voice. Turning, he dug into his saddlebags, obtained a packet of some sort, and then crossing to the house, entered. Cass was a squat, huskily-built man in a rumpled business suit.

"Where's the boys?" Jared asked.

"Stayed over the night for a little hell raising. I come on by myself. Don't like packing all this money around. Wish't the boss would pick somebody else to do the selling for him."

"Picked you 'cause you sort of look like a cattleman," Jared said. "Expect you could use a bite to eat."

Cass nodded, sat down to the table. "Ain't had nothing since morning. . . . Got some more beef in the corral, I see."

"Yeh. Boys better be showing up and tending to them. Boss don't like having stock on the place too long."

"They'll be here, come daylight. He been around lately?"

Jared was bending over the stove. "Not for a

week or so."

"He's got it mighty nice," Cass said with a heavy sigh. "Living in town, taking it easy, us doing all the hard work."

"We're getting paid good. Ain't no cause to complain. Got to remember he's the one that set this deal up, keeps it going."

Cass stirred, pulled the packet he'd taken from the saddlebags out of an inner coat pocket, dropped it on the table. Holt looked at it closely. It was a leather billfold.

"Had I any guts I'd hang onto this and head out for Mexico. Better'n a thousand dollars there this time. . . ."

"Money wouldn't last long," Jared said, setting a plate of food in front of the rider. "And you wouldn't neither. He'd have somebody on your trail before the sun was down."

"One day he maybe'll get just that chance," Cass said, staring morosely at the plate. "I'm getting a mite tired of—"

"Somebody coming," Jared broke in, drawing stiffly alert.

"The boys, I expect—"

"Can't be. Horses are on the canyon trail."

Immediately Cass pushed away from the table. He drew his pistol, stepped back into a corner out of sight. Jared picked up a shotgun, moved to the doorway.

Jim Holt shifted his attention to the far corner of the house. Three riders appeared, vague shadows on slowly walking mounts. Taut, he watched them cross the yard, halt at the rack. Relief and satisfaction rolled through him. He knew them all and they were not—as he had feared—Dave Bogard and his partners, but Reno, Billy Jay Austin, and Earl Munger.

"It's all right," Jared said over his shoulder, and then to the newcomers, "You all bring me that bottle?"

"Sure we did," Reno replied, holding aloft a quart bottle of whiskey. "Ain't never forgot you yet, have we?"

Jared held the screen open for the men to enter. "Nope, but there's always a first time—and a man can get powerful lonesome on a job like this."

Cass had emerged from his corner, was settling down again at the table. He glanced up at the three men, squinted for a better look.

"What the hell happened to you birds?"

Even from this distance Holt could see the swollen, discolored areas on the riders' faces. Another question solved.

"Had ourselves a peck of fun last night," Reno said, uncorking the bottle. "We worked over that fancy gunhand the ranchers hired on."

"Looks more like he worked you over," Jared observed.

"He did give us a tussle," Billy Jay drawled. "Hit me so hard once my head went around in a circle. But I reckon—"

"What gunhand?" Cass interrupted.

"Name of Holt. Ranchers hired him."

"Boss know about this?"

"Sure he knows," Reno said with a wave of his hand.

"He ain't worried none. Anyway, I expect he's rode off, left the country by now after what we done to him. Fact is, we ain't seen him since."

Cass began to eat in thoughtful silence as the bottle made the rounds. After a time he shook his head.

"Don't like it. Never heard of no range detective named Holt, but I'm betting that's what he is."

"He ain't no detective."

"Well, he's some kind of law. And if he's doing some looking around, he just might turn up something."

"Not if he's done gone."

"How do you know he is? Beating him up wasn't very smart. Should've used a gun on him."

"Earl and Billy Jay tried that, only they run into some bad luck."

Holt's jaw tightened. One more problem answered. It had been Reno and his two sidekicks all the way. . . . But four men had jumped him that night near the bunkhouse. Who was the missing rider—and who was the "Boss" they kept referring to?

Cass swore. "You're doing a good job of messing things up, that's for sure. Less ruckus you stir up, the better for all of us."

"Aw, there ain't nothing to get so riled about. Everything's going just the way we want. Ranchers all figure it's that bunch of jailbirds doing the rustling. Stashing them calves in that box canyon on their range plumb cooked their goose."

Holt nodded slowly to himself. He had the whole story now except for the identity of the fourth man involved in the fight, and the name of the rustling gang's leader—the "Boss." When he had that. . . .

"Maybe so," Cass said, "but I still aim to talk to the boss about it—about the way things are going."

Munger, silent through it all, said, "When'll that be?"

"Tomorrow. Going to rest my tail a bit, then ride on tonight. Sooner I get shed of this money, better I'll like it."

Munger glanced at Joe Reno and the young Texan. "You see him, tell him for us we're needing a raise. Job ain't no cinch like it once was. We ought to be getting better pay."

"I'll tell him," Cass said. "How about a few hands of cards?"

"Sounds good," Jared said, and added slyly, "You aim to use some of the cash you're toting in that wallet?"

"Hell, no!" Cass said instantly. "And don't you go saying something like that again! Boss just might start to wondering."

Jared grinned and Reno scratched at his chin stubble. "He's sure got you baffaloed."

"Ain't that atall. Just happens I know which end of a steer's got the horns. Aim to keep it that way."

Jim Holt watched the men settle down at the table. He'd been right about Reno and the two other members of McClendon's crew. He had thought Cully Ryan was mixed up in it, too—and the odds were still good that he was. His duties as Circle X ramrod would restrict his movements somewhat and would explain his not being with the others at that moment.

There was no overlooking the fact that four men had

been in the party that attacked him, and he was sure he had recognized Ryan's voice. Could it be that Cully had been an innocent member of the party, involved only because of injured feelings and pride, and deftly made use of by Joe Reno and his two friends?

It was possible—and it would come out later. The important thing was that he knew who was doing the cattle rustling, how it was being done, and where the gang based their operations. All he need do was draw his pistol, move up the door of the kitchen quietly, and take over, make prisoners of them all.

That would be a mistake. . . .

Holt realized that a moment later. He would have the rustlers, yes—at least most of them, including the three Circle X crew members who were so skillfully stripping the Jicarilla Basin while all the time being in the employ of the largest rancher in the area—but he still wouldn't have the head man, the leader, the brains behind it all.

The "Boss," as they called him, either being careful to never mention a name after having been so instructed, or simply using the term from force of habit. He evidently lived in Butte as Cass had expressed a determination to ride on that very night, meet with him in the morning, and deliver the cash received from the sale of the most recent batch of stolen stock.

He could put his hands on Reno and the others whenever he wished, Jim decided, now that he knew their identities. It was the man known as the "Boss" who was still in the shadows—and he, actually, was the most important of all.

Forget making prisoners of the men in the cabin. Grab them later. They were only hired hands in the operation. Just hang back, wait; when Cass rode on to meet with this mysterious "Boss," follow. He would then know who was at the head of the gang and be in a position to end the rustling in the Jicarilla Basin once and for all.

❆ XV ❆

THE POKER GAME was breaking up. Holt, dozing in the shadows behind the shed, came alive at the sudden, harsh sound of chair legs scraping across the bare floor of the kitchen. He'd been waiting three or four hours, he guessed.

Cass moved into view, flung wide the sagging screen door, and stepped out onto the landing. Joe Reno, followed by Munger and Billy Jay, trailed after him. All sauntered lazily to their mounts.

"You taking the canyon trail?" Reno asked, yawning as he swung to the saddle.

Cass said, "Nope, out of my way. Cutting around the end of the buttes is shorter. You ain't in no hurry, I'd be obliged for the company."

"Got to get back on the job before sunup," Reno explained. "Need to keep everybody thinking we're riding herd all night. . . . Don't be forgetting to tell the boss what Munger said."

"Sure, sure," Cass mumbled and climbed onto his horse.

The men separated, Reno and his two companions cutting around the north side of the house and heading for the canyon, Cass wheeling about and taking a course opposite that pointed him in a southeasterly direction.

Jim waited until all were well out of hearing, and then throwing a glance at Jared absently shuffling cards at the table, moved back to where the sorrel was tied. Jerking the leathers free, he mounted and rode after Cass.

He moved with care, holding the gelding to a fast walk, keeping to the darkness and endeavoring to avoid the open spaces on the hard ground where a hoof might set up an echo. Within a quarter hour he caught sight of the outlaw and settled back for a patient pursuit.

He was on a trail that was unfamiliar to him—one that led to Butte, of course—but he felt it necessary to keep Cass in sight. The man could turn off somewhere, and staying close to him until he reached his destination was all important now.

As Holt rode steadily on through the night, he thought of the scraps of information he'd overheard while listening to the men in the cabin. The rustling had been set up to operate in a most business-like manner, and evidently it was paying off handsomely. Whoever it was that headed up the deal—the "Boss," as they called him—was undoubtedly piling up a small fortune.

But there were some cracks beginning to appear in the wall; Munger and Reno and Billy Jay, the ones who did the actual rustling in the Basin, were getting rest-less, wanting more money. . . . The same applied to Cass, if conclusions could be drawn from what he had said to Jared.

Cass was the front man, the one who passed himself off as the cattle grower, met with the buyers, and nego-tiated the sales. Afterwards came the responsibility of carrying the money—in cash since to accept a draft that subsequently had to be presented at a bank might prove embarrassing as well as incriminating—and turning it over to the "Boss."

Jared, too, was uttering sounds of discontent, although not as noticeably as the others. The lonely job of staying on the premises day after day, night after night, having little to do most of the time, was begin-ning to wear on his nerves.

There would be periods of a week or more, probably, when there'd be no cattle to feed and water—stretches of silence when Reno and Munger and Billy Jay had yet to arrive with a stolen herd, and the rest of the gang was away, either on a drive or simply waiting around at a railhead while Cass consummated a deal.

The hours would weigh heavily upon Jared at such times, and he would no doubt be thinking of town, dreaming of a place like Butte with its lights and noisy saloons full of women, plenty of whiskey, gam-bling. . . .

He was breaking the thing wide open at just the right moment, Holt thought. A few more weeks, possibly even days, and the gang could split apart, the men scatter and go their separate ways—and then he would have done a lot of work and spent a lot of time for nothing.

The night wore on and Cass never varied from the steady, plodding pace to which he held his horse. More than likely he was asleep on the saddle, and since he had probably covered the same trail several times, the horse he rode knew it from memory and would not stray.

So, it had been Billy Jay and Earl Munger who had tried bushwhacking him the night he was returning from Bogard's. He had been certain, of course, that the riders had been members of the rustling gang; but at that time he had not linked clearly in his mind the three members of the Circle X crew to the outlaws. The pieces of the puzzle all fit now, however.

Holt smiled to himself. They thought he was out of it—that the beating they'd handed him in the dark had filled him with a fear for his life and sent him on his way. It was easy to see how they'd reached such a conclusion. No one at McClendon's had seen him since breakfast that following morning; and then later, after talking with Damion King's two hired hands, he'd ridden into the brakes and dropped out of sight.

He was going to enjoy those moments when he came face to face with Reno, Munger and the young Texan. And, yes—Cully Ryan, too. He was still convinced the Circle X ramrod had been one of the four men who had jumped him, and all other arguments notwithstanding, it was only logical to assume he was in on the rustling, too.

If Cully wasn't—if he'd simply been led on by his

personal feelings to throw in with Reno and his pals, and all the time was permitting them to carry on their rustling under his very nose while they masqueraded as friends and admirers—then he was dumber than a man should be, and Wade McClendon could have done better when he hired a foreman.

The first yellow flare of dawn was spraying above the eastern horizon. Light would come quickly now, and Holt knew he'd have to use greater care in not letting Cass spot him. He glanced around at the brightening country. He was somewhere south of Bogard's, presently following a trail that cut its way along the base of a lengthy butte.

Nothing was particularly familiar at that point, but a time later, with the sun out and well on its climb into the clean blue of the sky, his glance took in a landmark well to his left and he knew where he was.

Shortly, the trail he was on would join with the one he'd taken that morning out of Butte when he discovered the calves hidden on Dave Bogard's range. He felt better with that knowledge. It would be easy now to keep on Cass's heels and still stay far enough behind so as not alarm the man.

He could, if he wished, cut off and make a hurried ride to the Oatman place to have a quick talk with Bogard and his partners. He could explain what he had discovered, tell them they were in the clear—ask them to ride over and keep an eye on Jared and the D Bar K cattle he was looking after.

Dave Bogard would probably tell him to go to hell, that he wasn't interested in doing any favors for the ranchers in the Jicarilla Basin. They had been relegated to the status of outcasts, objects of suspicion for every outlaw act that had been committed in the area. Why should they lift a finger to help?

Jim reckoned he couldn't blame them for feeling that way. And he guessed there was no real need to stand watch on the rustlers' camp. Like as not, the herd they were holding would not be ready to move for another day, and by that time he'd have a dozen riders from the Basin ranches moving in to take over.

Butte. . . .

Jim pulled in behind a clump of brush at the edge of the last rock shoulder, waiting while Cass crossed a strip of open ground and turned into the end of the street. The outlaw was lost to view almost at once as he passed beyond the last building in the near row, and nudging the sorrel, Holt hurried to the corner of that structure.

Cass rode straight down the center of the dusty lane, paying no mind to the few mid-morning shoppers abroad, and pulled up finally at the hitchrail in front of the Palace Saloon.

As he swung off his horse, Holt sent the sorrel moving toward that building. He'd had thoughts about Jess Hammer, the new owner of the saloon, had wondered about the evident prosperity of the place. Hammer could very easily be the boss of the rustlers.

Leaving the gelding at the side of the structure, Holt stepped up on the porch, crossed to the doorway, and looked in. Cass was standing at the bar having himself a drink. The same man was behind the counter, and there appeared to be no one else around.

The outlaw finished his drink, laid a coin on the bar and wheeled about. Holt drew back hastily, trapped on the landing, and assumed a slouched, shoulders-to-the-wall stance. Cass came into the open, the black leather fold plainly visible in his hip pocket, and giving no attention to Jim, crossed the street to the hotel.

Jim watched the man disappear into the double doorway of the two-storied building and immediately followed, again halting just outside. He could see the rustler at the desk speaking with the clerk. Whatever question Cass asked of the balding, little man drew a negative shake of the head. The outlaw spun, came back through the lobby and returned to the street.

Holt watched him move back to his horse, mount up, and head north along the street. It could mean only one thing; whoever he sought was not in town and he was going now to find him.

Impatience stirred Jim. The game of hide and seek was beginning to tire, wear thin. Maybe he should just ride up to Cass, collar him and bring an end to the chase, depend upon forcing information as to the identity of the rustler boss from him later. But such could run into time—time in which the leader of the gang, hearing of Cass's arrest, could escape. No, best to keep following. . . .

He returned to the sorrel, and doubling back to the alley behind the west row of buildings so as to avoid any possible interruptions on the part of Marshal Pete Hornbuckle or anyone else, made his way to the far end of the street. Cass was just disappearing behind the brush bordering the road that led to the Basin.

Frowning, Holt hurried on, keeping the ragged growth of rabbitbush, sage, and scrub cedars between the outlaw and himself. Was the man he needed to find someone in the Basin—one of the ranchers? He smiled grimly. It was possible. He'd run into strange deals like this before. But perhaps he was drawing conclusions too soon. Cass could be planning to swing off the road, head for some cabin or place entirely unknown.

But the outlaw did not swerve from the well-marked road. And Holt, forced by the contours of the land, had swung the sorrel up onto the dusty course and was trailing at a respectable distance.

Not once did the rustler look back, evidently sure of himself and of where he was going. Holt kept doggedly at it, prepared for anything, everything; and then an hour later when they reached the fork in the road where the branch to the left led off to the Circle X, he came to a full stop.

Cass was heading for Wade McClendon's ranch.

❋ XVI ❋

JIM HOLT stared after the slowly diminishing figure of the outlaw. Shock and disbelief was rolling through him as the full implication of the man's intentions registered on his mind.

Wade McClendon mixed up in the rustling that was plaguing the Jicarilla Basin? The whole idea was ridiculous. McClendon had no need—no reason—for such. Then who?

Cully Ryan. . . . That had to be the answer, and it was easily possible. Ryan's hostility had been evident from the start; he ran with the three men that definitely were part of the rustling gang—and the possibility that he had been one of the participants in the fight behind the bunkhouse was strong. Cully Ryan . . . sure. Yet Munger had spoken to Cass as if he seldom saw the leader of the outlaws, had even requested him to put in a word for a larger slice of the profits. That made no sense; likely Munger as well as Reno and Billy Jay encountered Ryan every day. . . . Then who—

Cass was fading into the trees along the Jicarilla River. Holt touched the sorrel with his spurs, set him to an easy lope and resumed his pursuit of the man. A short time later he again had the outlaw in sight, angling now across the narrow flat west of the stream and moving toward the gate leading into McClendon's yard.

Jim took no pains now to keep back and out of sight. Cass, upon seeing him, would believe only that he was a Circle X rider coming in for some reason or another. He reached the gate at the moment the outlaw halted at the rack in front of the main house, slowed to give the man time to cross the porch and knock on the door, and then guided the gelding up to the side of the structure.

Dropping from the saddle, Jim moved to the end of the gallery. He had a glimpse of McClendon standing in the doorway, holding the screen back for Cass to enter. Doubts again assailed Jim Holt, but he remained motionless, giving the rancher time to turn to his guest.

One thing was certain; Cass was not there to see Cully Ryan. He would have headed for the bunkhouse, or made inquiry of some of the help and ridden out onto the range to locate the foreman.

Disturbed, his features hard-cornered from the indisputable facts that were shaping up before him, Holt stepped up onto the porch, started for the door. He halted in stride as a rider pounded into the yard.

The man was yelling something, the words lost in the thudding of his horse's hoofs, while he waved his arms wildly above his head. Punchers came pouring from the bunkhouse, some only partly dressed. Others appeared from back of the corrals and the barn. Cully Ryan emerged from the kitchen, a cup of coffee in his hand, and walked hurriedly out into the center of the hardpack.

"Whoa!" he shouted at the rider. "Slow down, Amos! What's this all about?"

The man on the lathered horse veered to where the foreman stood. He swept off his hat, wiped the sweat from his leathery face.

"All hell's busted loosed!" he said. "King and Bevan got themselves a posse together. Heading for the Oatman place. Aim to string up them jailbirds!"

A tautness gripped Jim Holt. He started to wheel, mount the sorrel and strike out for Bogard's when Wade McClendon's voice, coming from behind him, pulled him up short.

"What's that?"

Amos repeated his words. "Could be 'most there by now," he added. "I run accrost them down in the south pasture. Was moving right along—about a dozen men."

McClendon swore. "Was bound to come, I suppose. Finding those calves—"

Holt pivoted to the rancher. "They're not guilty of that—or anything else!" he snarled. "Tracked down the real rustlers last night. Cabin, corral, even the last bunch of steers King lost, found them all in little valley west of the brakes."

McClendon's eyes spread with surprise. "You know who, the rustlers are?"

"Some of them, not all." He eyed the rancher closely. "I know enough—but it'll have to wait. We've got to get to Bogard's, stop that lynching party."

McClendon bobbed his head crisply, crossed to the edge of the porch. "Cully!" he shouted. "Get every man on the place mounted up!" Pivoting, he glanced at Holt as he hurried toward the doorway. "Be with you in a couple of minutes."

Holt dropped from the porch, the question of Cass and the man he'd come to see temporarily sidetracked by the emergency. The sorrel was about done in, and in no condition for further use that day. Seizing the reins, he hurried the gelding to the first corral, and stripping his gear, threw it on the most likely-looking of the available mounts—a tall bay. Close by, Circle X men were also saddling, talking excitedly back and forth.

The bay ready, Jim mounted. He cut across to where Ryan and several others were beginning to assemble and await McClendon. The foreman, he saw, had a crushed lip, and there was a swelling below his left eye. . . . Right again.

"I'm going on ahead," he said to Ryan. "Tell McClendon."

Cully nodded stiffly and Jim spurred away, leaving the yard at a fast gallop. Another ten or fifteen minutes delay incurred in waiting for the rancher could mean the difference in life or death for Dave Bogard and his partners.

And he would be responsible for it. That bitter thought filled his mind as, hunched low over the bay, he raced across the rolling plains toward the Oatman place. He'd been the one to find the calves, thus throwing fuel onto the fires of suspicion that were smoldering in the Basin.

Bogard, Wright and the *vaquero*, Nestor Delgado, were guilty of nothing other than trying to live right, make a go of a hopelessly poor ranch—one that at best stood only a slim chance of succeeding no matter how hard they tried. And he was robbing them of even that—perhaps even of life itself—unless he could get there in time.

He looked ahead. Bogard's was just beyond the next rise, no more than two or three miles distant. Jim threw his glance to the right. The lynching party would be moving in from that point. There was no sign of them. Either they had already crossed the ridge or he had managed, by angling across the range, to get in front of them.

But that was hardly possible. Figuring the time it took Amos to ride in after seeing the party, and then the few minutes lost in getting underway, it was only logical to assume the riders were ahead of him.

The clawing in his throat grew tighter, and he roweled the bay for more speed. The horse responded; his ears flattened, his long neck extended farther while his legs fairly churned as he swept up the slopes, down into the shallow valleys, and over the grassy saddles without faltering. Holt's jaw was set. He had to make it in time. He must get there, stop King and Bevan and the men with them before they could make a terrible mistake—one he felt was indirectly his own fault.

Smoke. . . .

A tremor shook Jim Holt when he saw the sudden rise of black, ugly streamers beyond the ridge. Bogard's house. . . . The lynch mob had set fire to it, were burning it to the ground. . . . It could mean he was too late.

An oath ripped from his lips. He began to lash the bay with the ends of the reins, goad with his spurs, shout in an effort to get more speed. And then suddenly he was pitching forward and the bay was collapsing under him as the crack of a rifle filled his ears.

❊ XVII ❊

HE HIT THE GROUND HARD, went piling into a clump of tough mountain mahogany. He was stunned but instinct kept him moving, sent him rolling frantically to one side as his hand clawed out the pistol on his hip.

The rifle barked again, the sound coming from the trees to his left. He saw two riders burst suddenly from the shadows, fired twice at them as the rifle spoke once more.

Dirt sprayed over him and there was a vicious clipping sound in the brush behind him as bullets slashed through the leaves. He dodged to one side; reversed, gained the shelter of a thick-trunked pine tree.

The two riders had slipped again into the dense brush, their weapons silent. Holt looked to the bay. The big horse lay flat, neck doubled, blood seeping from his head. He had died before he was down.

Grim, anger flaming through him, Holt fully realized that someone was determined he'd not reach the Oatman place in time to save Bogard and his partners. He crouched behind the pine and searched the undergrowth for the two who had stopped him, held him back. Their very presence, although unseen, kept him pinned down and helpless. The hell with that! He had to force their hand, bring them into the open.

Reloading quickly, he looked around, located another tree of sufficient size to afford protection. It was a long ten yards away, but it offered the only course of action left to him—and every minute counted.

Taking a deep breath, Holt leaped into the clear, dashed for the pine. Instantly the rifles began to crackle. Jim threw himself flat, steadied, and using both hands to hold his pistol firmly, fired at the partly-hidden figure he could now see at the edge of the brush.

The bushwhacker jolted, stumbled forward, fell. Earl Munger! It was no surprise to Jim Holt. He had suspected it would be Reno's crowd who had lain in ambush. But he was giving it no thought, his mind occupied instead with the necessity for staying alive, getting his gunsights lined up on the second man.

Second? There should be three . . . Reno, Billy Jay and Munger. A coolness came over Holt. Best play it careful. He'd thought he was dealing with two killers—had actually seen only two. The third could be holding back, wanting to give him that impression, just waiting to make his move.

Flat on the ground behind a rotting log, he scanned the brush where Munger had been hiding. At least one more rifleman was in there, too. The third, if there was a third man, must be somewhere close by. He could see no sign of him, however; no shadow, no slight movement.

Holt turned his head to the side. The pine tree was still half a dozen strides away, but again the only solution to a standoff was motion on his part. Drawing his legs under him, he sprang upright, spun, and lunged for the protection of the tree behind which he first had found safety.

The ruse worked. Reversing his course had confused the hidden rifleman. He stepped hurriedly into the open, weapon lifted. Holt slammed a bullet into him as he was wheeling, saw the rider sink to one knee and the rifle fall from his hands.

"Don't shoot!" the rider yelled.

It was the young Texan, Billy Jay Austin. The bullet had struck him in the leg, the impact knocking him down, jarring him loose from his weapon. He was out of the fight, but Holt was not forgetting the third man—Joe Reno.

"All right!" he called from behind the safety of the tree. "Tell Reno to throw down his gun and step out where I can see him, or I'll put a slug through your head!"

"He ain't here!" Austin answered.

Holt snapped a shot at the outlaw. The bullet spewed dirt over his legs. He yelled, drew back.

"It's the truth—he ain't here! Was only me and Earl waiting."

"Where the hell is he?"

"Up with them others at the Oatman place. Told me and Earl to stay here just in case you come along."

Jim sent another bullet into the soil alongside the rustler, causing him to flinch.

"I'm not lying—"

"You'd better not be," Holt warned, stepping from behind the pine. "I'm holding a bead on your head. If Reno shows up, you'll be the first to die."

"I'm telling you, he ain't here," Austin mumbled doggedly.

Hurrying, Jim moved to the outlaw's side. Austin was speaking the truth, he felt certain now, and he had no time to lose. Reaching down, he jerked the Texan's pistol from its holster, threw it into the brush.

"On your feet!"

Billy Jay shook his head. "Can't. You done busted my leg—"

"You're getting on your horse just the same," Holt snarled. Holstering his own weapon, he caught the outlaw under the shoulders and helped him to where his horse waited. Boosting the man onto the saddle, he led Austin's mount to where Munger's was tied.

"What're you aiming to do with me?" Billy Jay asked.

"We're joining that lynch mob," Holt answered, mounting. "Could be it'll be you they'll end up using a rope on."

"Me? What're you trying to do? Make it look like I've been—"

"Better start saving up your breath," Jim said. "Happens I know the whole thing—that it's been you, Reno, Munger, Cass, Jared, and a few others doing the cattle stealing."

Austin's jaw sagged. He stirred on his saddle, winced, grabbed at his leg as pain shot through him.

"Paid that shack west of the ridge a little visit last night," Holt said, wheeling his horse around. "Heard all that was said. Know just how you pulled off the rustling, changed the brands in that chute, then drove the stock south where Cass sold them."

"You was there last night?" Billy Jay's voice was high, cracked.

"I was. Only thing I don't know is who the head man is—the one you all call the 'Boss.' Who is he?"

Austin's mouth snapped shut. "Then you don't know nothing, for sure," he said after a moment.

"Know enough to hang you and Reno, along with Cass and Jared. Leave it up to you—I've got no time to waste. You can answer now or when they start stringing you up."

Billy Jay shook his head. "You're so goddam smart finding out things—find that out, too."

"Suit yourself," Holt said brusquely, unwilling to delay any longer. "Get out in front of me and ride for the Oatman place. You try anything, I'll blast you off that saddle!"

❋ XVIII ❋

IN THE TANGLED GROWTH AND ROCKS a quarter mile short of Bogard's, Holt surged forward and drew abreast Billy Jay.

"Pull up!" he shouted.

Immediately the outlaw reined in. Jim leaped from the saddle, and dragging the man roughly from his horse, half pushed, half carried him into a well-screened pocket of brush.

"What the hell you figuring on doing?" the Texan demanded.

"Shut up!" Holt snapped, ripping off his bandana and using it as a gag across the rustler's mouth. "You're staying here. And you'd better pray I don't get to that lynch mob too late."

Jerking off his belt, he bound Austin's hands behind his back, and then mounting Munger's horse again, hurried on toward the smoke plumes towering into the sky.

He counted twenty men in the party as he crossed the open ground and rode onto the hardpack: Jack Bevan, King, Joe Reno, and a number of other riders from the ranches. All appeared to be just waiting.

The house was down to its rock foundation, its thin, heat-dried walls and furnishings having gone up in flames quickly. There was no sign of Dave Bogard and his two partners, and that immediately eased the tension within Holt. Evidently the mob had been unable to find the men. Giving Reno a cold glance, Jim rode up to the half circle of punchers, placed his attention upon King and Bevan.

"This is a mistake," he said quietly.

"The hell it is!" Damion King shot back angrily. "We should've done this months ago! Would've, too, if—"

"Here comes the Circle X bunch," a voice cut in.

Jack Bevan straightened on his saddle. "Good. McClendon ought to have a hand in this."

Holt faced the oncoming riders: McClendon, Cully Ryan, other Circle X punchers. Reece Oatman was also in the crowd. This stirred a brief wonder in Holt until he recalled the man's telling him he'd been invited to the McClendons' for a meal. Apparently this was the day.

His eyes drifted on, probing persistently, and then he relaxed. Cass was also there. Kneeing his horse about, Jim moved forward a few paces to meet the men.

"We get here in time?" McClendon asked, pulling up. His glance took in the charred remains of the house as he swiped at the sweat on his face. "They in there?"

Holt studied the rancher through narrowed eyes. He shook his head. "Expect they're hid out, holed up somewhere. Makes no difference. We won't need them."

"What's that?" Damion King barked, spurring

in closer.

"Said we don't need Bogard and the men with him, at least not right now. Need them later so's they can collect damages from you for burning down their property."

"Now, just a goddam minute—"

"Holt claims he's found the real rustlers," McClendon broke in. "I want to hear him out."

Joe Reno laughed. "You can bet it'll be everybody but them three jailbird friends of his'n."

Jim favored the outlaw with a humorless smile. He had most of the answers, but he was still uncertain as to the final—and most important—factor. But the door to that was open now. He shifted his attention to Cass, leveled a finger at him.

"You. Mind coming over here?"

The outlaw frowned, glanced around, and then rode forward into the center of the riders where Holt waited.

"I'm here. What're you wanting?"

"Everybody take a good look at this man," Jim said. "He a friend of anyone?"

A murmur of noes ran through the crowd. Holt cast a sideways look at Joe Reno. He, too, was shaking his head. So was Cully Ryan. Joe was lying, of course; Jim was yet uncertain about Cully. He shifted his eyes to Wade McClendon.

"How about you?"

The rancher shrugged. "Don't recollect ever seeing him before today."

Cass was sitting quietly on his horse, eyes empty, face expressionless.

"Seems funny," Holt said. "Rode up to your place, knocked on the door, and you let him in."

McClendon shrugged, scratched at his jaw. "Sure. He was looking for Oatman. Had some papers to deliver. Been in town and somebody'd told him Reece was out to my place for dinner."

✖ XIX ✖

OATMAN! REECE OATMAN! Everything fell into place in a single, flashing instant. Oatman, failing as a rancher, had taken another road to wealth. He'd organized his gang of rustlers, arranged for its operation, and by chance had found the perfect out in Bogard, Wright, and Nestor Delgado, if and when things went wrong.

"What're you driving at?" King demanded. "All this palavering makes no sense. We damn well know who's doing the rustling—"

"You don't," Holt said flatly, shifting around to where he faced Oatman and McClendon head on. With a slight, swift motion of his arm, he drew his pistol and let it hang there, leveled at no one in particular.

"Wade," he said, "those papers—delivered to Oatman—they were in a leather fold. Take a look at it. You'll find money, not papers. There'll be somewhere around a thousand dollars."

The rancher stared, turned to Oatman. "I don't know what he's getting at, Reece, but I reckon I'll have to do what he says."

Oatman drew up in stiff outrage. "What's the matter

with all of you? A man's got rights. I don't have to submit to no search—"

"You do," Jim cut in softly, "unless you want a bullet through your head. Happens I was in that valley west of the brakes last night—the place where you've got a cabin and a corral for your crew of rustlers to work out of."

The hush that dropped over the men in the yard was broken only by an occasional pop in the still-smoldering embers of the fire.

"Heard plenty," Holt continued. "Then followed Cass to town when he said he was taking the money for the last batch of stolen stock in to the man they called the 'Boss'. . . . That's you, Oatman."

Oatman's face wore a fixed smile. "Why, that's crazy, *loco*. I never—"

"Let's see that wallet," McClendon said, his manner now hard and cold. "Seems all the proof we're needing is there. If Holt's wrong, like you say—"

"The hell with you!" Oatman shouted and grabbed for his pistol.

Cully Ryan, close by, struck out with his fist, caught Oatman on the side of the head. In the same breath, he yelled, "Look out, Holt!"

Jim caught Joe Reno's motion from the tail of his eye. He buckled forward, triggered his weapon in the same instant that the outlaw fired. Reno's bullet *spanged* against the saddle horn, went screaming off into space as everything in the yard was a sudden, dusty confusion of milling horses, shouting men, and gunsmoke.

Holt, crouched low, had not taken his eyes from Reno. The outlaw was a dim figure in the haze, sliding slowly off his saddle, arms rigid at his sides. Abruptly he fell to the ground.

Jim turned then to the crowd, aware of more shouts coming from the lower end of the clearing. Cully Ryan was holding a gun on Cass. Another rider had the muzzle of his rifle pressed deep into Reece Oatman's back. McClendon, Damion King, and Jack Bevan were examining the leather billfold, thumbing through a sheaf of currency.

All looked up as Holt moved in close. McClendon nodded. "Like you said, little over a thousand dollars here. How'd you—"

"Already told you. Found the cabin where they work over the stock they rustle. King, those fifty steers you lost are there and probably getting their brands changed right about now. Place is due west of here."

The cattleman frowned. "West? Hell, a man can't drive stock—"

"They did. Reno, Earl Munger, and Billy Jay Austin. They hired out to McClendon, but worked for Oatman."

An oath exploded from Wade McClendon's lips. "Them dirty, thieving bastards! When I lay me hands on the other two I'll—"

"Too late for Munger. You'll find him dead back in the Basin. I've got Billy Jay tied up in the brush at the edge of the clearing." Holt paused, glanced to Ryan. "Sort of had you pegged for a member of the gang, too—way you strung along with them."

Cully looked down, wagged his head. "I was about four kinds of a damned fool. They suckered me into jumping you. Teaching you a lesson, they claimed."

"That's what had me guessing, knowing you were in on that."

"What's this?" McClendon demanded. "Something I ain't been told about?"

"Not important," Holt said, and looking toward the riders approaching from the lower end of the yard, nodded to King and Jack Bevan. "Here come the men you were in such a hurry to string up. I figure you owe them more than an apology."

Immediately Bevan said, "You're right, and I'm ready to admit it."

"Same here," Damion King added. "And while I'm trying to set myself square with them, I'll appreciate your telling my boys how to find those steers."

"Be glad to," Jim said. "They hurry right along, they should be in time to get back your stock and nail all the rest of Oatman's gang."

THE CELLS in Butte's jail were packed. What with Oatman, Billy Jay, Cass, Jared, and the three men captured when the ranchers' men went over the ridge and closed in on the rustlers' camp, Marshal Pete Hornbuckle's quarters were bulging at the joints.

"Offering you the lawman job again," McClendon said to Holt as they stood in the street fronting the jail. "Place is getting too big to do without."

"You've got one," Jim replied. "Don't need another."

"Old Pete? Hell, he ain't no real lawman."

"Could be if you'd all get behind him. No marshal's any better than the people backing him. Not saying he's any Wild Bill Hickok, but he can handle most of what he's apt to run into around here if he knows you're standing by him—not treating him as a joke."

McClendon shrugged, not fully sold. "Well, maybe you're right. Leastwise, we can give it a try. . . . Obliged to you, Jim, for coming when I sent for you."

"Glad it all worked out. You ever need me again, just holler."

"Fine. Whereabouts you headed now?"

Holt looked out across the smooth hills. "First off, I'm riding out to Bogard's. Dave and his partners have about got their new house built. King and the others sent some of the hired hands over to help. Figure to just hang around there a few days, take it easy."

"Then?"

Jim Holt swung onto the sorrel, grinned down at the rancher. *"Quien sabe?"* he said, and rode on.

Center Point Publishing
600 Brooks Road ● PO Box 1
Thorndike ME 04986-0001 USA

(207) 568-3717

US & Canada:
1 800 929-9108